SPECIAL FORCES CADETS

ASSASSIN

Special Forces Cadets

CHRIS RYAN

SPECIAL FORCES CADETS

ASSASSIN

HOT
KEY
BOOKS

First published in Great Britain in 2021 by
HOT KEY BOOKS
80–81 Wimpole St, London W1G 9RE
Owned by Bonnier Books
Sveavägen 56, Stockholm, Sweden
www.hotkeybooks.com

A CIP catalogue record for this book is available from the British Library.

ISBN: 978-1-4714-0790-1
Also available as an ebook and in audio

1

This book is typeset using Atomik ePublisher
Printed and bound in Great Britain by Clays Ltd, Elcograf S.p.A.

Hot Key Books is an imprint of Bonnier Books UK
www.bonnierbooks.co.uk

≋ SPECIAL FORCES CADETS ≋

1

The Dissident

'That's a school?'

It was a cold day in late November. Five teenagers sat side by side in a large room on the first floor of Valley House, staring at an interactive whiteboard. Their names were Max, Abby, Lukas, Lili and Sami. They wore camouflage trousers, sturdy Gore-Tex boots and tight-fitting base layers. It was cold outside and in, but they showed no sign of feeling it. The Special Forces Cadets were acclimatised to their bleak, spartan surroundings: to this solitary house nestled in an inaccessible valley. To the elements that offered every type of extreme weather except sunshine.

The whiteboard showed a bird's-eye view of an ancient, sprawling building, all turrets and quads, under a thick layer of snow.

'Seriously? That's a *school*?' It was Abby who repeated the question. She had pale skin and blue eyes. Her hair was thick, brown and messy. She wore a double cartilage piercing in her left ear and fiddled with it as she spoke.

'Yup,' said the oldest of the three adults facing them. His name was Hector and he was dressed in black. Dark hair, dark beard, dark stare. Hector was the most senior of the three Watchers – the adults whose job it was to train, brief and protect the five Special Forces Cadets. And by some distance he was the most curmudgeonly.

'Looks more like a castle,' said Abby.

'Yeah. Don't forget your Harry Potter robes.'

It was so unusual for Hector to crack anything remotely resembling a joke that the cadets were momentarily silenced. After a few seconds, Abby gave him a sweet smile.

'Roger that, Dumbledore!' she said, earning herself a deep frown.

'It's got its own helipad?' Sami said, pointing at an area at the edge of the school grounds. He was a slight Syrian boy with brown eyes, dark skin and a perpetually earnest expression.

'Where else are the students' helicopters going to land?' said Angel, the only female Watcher. Her fiery red hair was pulled back into a tight ponytail. Her voice had a sarcastic edge. It was clear that she didn't approve of schools with helipads.

'Where I went to school,' Sami said, 'there wasn't even a playground. Come to think of it, there wasn't even a school, after the bombs came.'

Sami had been born and brought up on the streets of Syria, and orphaned by its brutal civil war. It was something they all had in common: being an orphan. If you wanted to join the Special Forces Cadets, it was a prerequisite.

'This isn't like any school in Syria,' said the third Watcher.

Woody had sandy hair, a friendly, open face and a nose that had clearly been badly broken in the past. 'This is the Zermatt Academy in Switzerland. Billionaires only need apply.'

'Sons and daughters of billionaires,' Lili said. 'There's a difference.' Lili was Chinese and comfortably the most intelligent of the cadets.

'Yeah,' Lukas agreed. 'A posh school for spoiled rich kids. What's that got to do with us?' Lukas was a black kid from Compton, Los Angeles, whose parents had been killed in gang violence. His brow was furrowed and he clearly looked as though he shared Angel's disdain for the hyper-rich students of the Zermatt Academy.

'Obvious, isn't it?' said Max Johnson quietly.

Max was the leader of their group. It wasn't an official thing. Nobody ever acknowledged it out loud. But it was true nonetheless. Max's leadership was not brash or showy; it was quiet and considered. When Max spoke, the others listened.

They were listening now, waiting for him to explain himself.

'I'm guessing the students at the Zermatt Academy come from all over the world. A bit like us. And if, for any reason, it's necessary to embed some agents on the school premises, a few extra students on campus would go unnoticed.'

Hector nodded. 'Right.' He tapped the whiteboard and the image changed to a photograph of a man in an open-necked shirt. He looked Middle Eastern, perhaps in his fifties, with round, rimless glasses and a balding head. 'Meet Barak Al Zarani. He's one of the world's leading nuclear scientists.'

'I don't say this lightly,' Angel interrupted, 'but there's a chance he might even be smarter than Lili.'

3

'He's smarter than almost everyone,' Hector said. 'He's Iranian. How much do you know about Iran's nuclear capability?'

'It's not what they'd like it to be,' Sami said, his expression grim.

'Exactly. For years now, Iran has wanted to become a nuclear power – that is, it has wanted nuclear weapons. So far, the international community has managed to stop it from happening, but Iran's getting closer. One of the reasons is, it has a group of talented nuclear scientists. Barak here is the best of them.'

'So he's the guy we have to thank when the world goes bang?' Lukas said.

'No. Six months ago, Barak Al Zarani fled Iran. He's what we call a dissident. He was under pressure from the Iranian government to accelerate their nuclear programme. He sought sanctuary in the UK, where he's able to use his expertise to develop renewable energy sources. If he has his way, he might be the guy we have to thank for saving the world, not destroying it.'

'I take it back,' Lukas muttered.

'What does this have to do with Switzerland?' Lili asked.

Hector tapped the screen again. Another face appeared. It was younger, but the features were similar: the brown eyes, the long nose. 'Barak's wife died ten years ago but he has a son. This is Darius. He fled Iran with his father. Now he goes to school . . .'

'. . . at the Zermatt Academy,' Max completed the sentence.

Hector nodded.

4

'I don't get it,' Lili said. 'He's a dissident scientist, not a billionaire. Why would he send his son there?'

'Simple,' said Hector. 'It's to keep him alive. When Barak fled to the UK, he bought his sanctuary with all the information he knew about the Iranian nuclear programme. That's not the kind of thing the Iranians want to encourage.'

'Do they want to kill him?' Sami asked, his eyes flashing.

'They probably wouldn't mind,' said Hector. 'But that wouldn't be their first option. They'd like to get Barak back to Iran, and the best way to do that . . .'

'. . . is to kidnap his son.' This time it was Abby's turn to interrupt the Watcher.

'Precisely,' said Hector. 'Darius is in a very precarious position.'

'I still don't see why that puts him at the Zermatt Academy,' said Max.

'He's there at Barak's insistence,' Hector said. 'Barak seems to think that, since Switzerland tries to stay neutral in international disputes, it's more difficult for Iran to launch a kidnap attempt on Swiss territory. He's wrong, but it's what he thinks.'

'Why don't the British just refuse to let Darius go there?'

Lili's eyes narrowed. 'Because they don't really want his dad to work on clean energy. They want him on hand in case they need help with their own nuclear weapons.'

The cadets looked at Hector, as though expecting him to confirm or deny Lili's theory.

'Politics is a messy business,' he said. 'Our job isn't to ask about the motives. Our job is to look after a young man who, through no fault of his own, could be in a lot of danger. The

British authorities have received intelligence that an attempt to kidnap Darius might be in the offing. If the Iranians can get him back to Iran, his father is likely to return. There's even a possibility that they might attempt to assassinate him, to discourage other dissidents from following Barak's lead. You're there to prevent either outcome. The second half of the term starts in two days. We deploy to London this afternoon. We'll overnight there before heading to Zermatt. We'll brief you further in transit.' Hector looked along the line of cadets. 'You lot need to get ready to go back to school.'

Abby sniffed. 'You know, professional assassins and kidnappers I can deal with. Mortal danger, not a problem. But please tell me I don't have to sit through another maths lesson. I haven't been to school for a long old time now, and I think it might be the end of me.' She looked genuinely pained at the idea.

'Don't worry,' Lili said, standing up and tossing her hair. 'I'll help you with your homework. Actually, I've kind of missed it.'

'Freak,' Lukas muttered as the rest of the cadets stood up and followed Lili out of the room.

Max was the last of the cadets to leave the room. He dawdled down the stairs. He did this because there was something on the ground floor of this house that he liked to spend a little time with – alone. It was a large oil painting over the fireplace in a dark, musty, oak-panelled room with squashy sofas and heavy curtains that were always kept closed. The other cadets seldom came in here, and Max thought he knew why: he was always pensive when he'd paid this picture a visit, and the others seemed to silently respect the room as his own.

He was thoughtful now as he stood in front of the fireplace and looked up at the painting. On the bottom edge of the frame was an oval panel etched with the letters *R.E.J.* The painting showed a man in full military dress, with brown hair parted on the right, thick eyebrows and a strong jawline. The man looked very like Max, which made sense, because it was his dad. Reg Johnson had founded the Special Forces Cadets. He had died, along with Max's mum, in Afghanistan. Max had no memory of them, just a few photos and this painting. He found it comforting to spend time with it – almost, but not quite, as if he was spending time with his dad.

He wondered if his dad had ever imagined that his own son would one day be part of this secret unit. The Special Forces Cadets existed to carry out dangerous missions where adults would be conspicuous but where youngsters would go unnoticed. Max's work with the cadets had put him in the path of terrorists and enemy soldiers, into seething, hissing jungles and bullet-strewn favelas. He'd been shot at and half drowned. He'd jumped out of aircraft and crawled through sewers. It had not, by any measure, been a normal childhood. Would his parents have wanted that for him? Max would never know.

There was a tap on the door. Abby was standing there. She and Max had saved each other's lives in the past – and had shared a kiss more than once. The other cadets had a habit of giving them space if they needed it, but their relationship had stalled. It often seemed to Max that they were too scared to let it flourish. After all, they knew how dangerous their lives were, how easy it would be for one of them to lose the other.

It was not like Abby to look diffident, but she did now. As if she felt she was intruding. 'Green Thunder's on its way,' she said.

Green Thunder was the name of the cadets' dedicated Chinook helicopter. It routinely ferried them from Valley House to wherever they needed to be. Abby was tactfully telling Max to get a move on.

'I'm coming,' he said, and walked towards her.

'Hey,' Abby said with a grin. 'Posh school in Zermatt. Snowboarding, hot chocolate – could be a laugh, huh?'

Max smiled. 'Sure,' he said. 'Could be dangerous too, what with all those kidnappers and assassins.'

'Ah well,' said Abby. 'We need something to keep us on our toes. We'd get lazy otherwise. Nothing like a few kidnappers and assassins to keep the blood pumping.'

'Right,' Max said. He looked over his shoulder and gave his dad one last glance. 'Come on, let's get moving before Hector starts barking at us.'

'Now there's something we can both agree on,' Abby said, and they strode quickly out of the house.

2

Bullies

Twenty-four hours later, Max stepped out onto the helipad of the Zermatt Academy.

The helipad had been cleared of snow, but there was powder a foot deep around its perimeter, which billowed into a stinging cloud of white as the rotor blades powered down. Max shielded his eyes with his forearm as he fought his way through the snow towards an elderly man who looked like a butler.

'This way please, Mr Johnson,' the man shouted over the noise of the chopper. 'I'll have somebody bring your luggage.'

The cadets were using their real names, but in the time between their briefing back at Valley House and their arrival in Zermatt, they had committed detailed individual back stories to memory. Max was the son of a tech billionaire who divided his time between Belgravia and Silicon Valley. He had been kicked out of three schools for neglecting his studies, and had finally been sent to the Zermatt Academy by his desperate parents. Was there, Max wondered, something in the demeanour of the old man leading him through the snow towards the grand old buildings of the school that suggested he knew Max was likely to be something of a handful? Max decided he needed to play his part.

'The helicopter was late,' he said sullenly.

'It's the weather, Mr Johnson,' said the man. 'There's a storm coming in. A bad one, by all accounts. The pilot had to be sure it was safe to fly.'

'It looked all right to me,' said Max. And it had. The helicopter ride from Geneva airport had been exhilarating. They had flown through clear skies over the snow-covered Alps. As they descended into Zermatt, the Matterhorn had loomed – threateningly and thrillingly – over them. Here on the ground, the air was biting but clear, cold in Max's lungs as he breathed deeply. The midday sky was a piercing blue.

'Things can change quickly in the mountains, young man. Especially at this time of year. We learn not to take the elements for granted.'

Max grunted, but made a mental note of that piece of advice as they walked across a snow-covered quad.

'I'm Cavendish,' said the man. 'School porter. I'll be showing you to your room. If you have any administrative queries, you can find me in the porter's lodge on the south side of the campus.'

'Porter's lodge,' Max said. 'Of course.' He looked around. There were high buildings on three sides, constructed from dark brown stone with tall leaded windows, turreted roofs and gargoyles along the ramparts. A few students milled around, dressed in expensive-looking ski jackets and sunglasses. They oozed wealth. It was Saturday, so nobody was in class, and Max felt the eyes of his fellow students on him. This place was grand and expensive, no doubt. But it didn't feel friendly.

Cavendish opened a heavy wooden door and led him inside. They entered an enormous oak-panelled entrance hall where a large fire burned in the grate. There was a grand staircase and four corridors leading from the room. Their footsteps echoed as they followed one of these corridors, which was long and brightly lit, with numbered doors on either side. After every third door on the left-hand side of the corridor was an alcove with a hanging rail. Each alcove was stuffed full of winter gear – coats, boots, waterproof trousers, all apparently left there to dry. They stopped outside the door marked '15'.

'This will be your room,' Cavendish said. 'Lunch is served at one o'clock, dinner at seven. I'll leave you to settle in.'

'Am I the only new arrival?' Max asked.

'As it happens, no. Two young ladies arrived this morning, and we're expecting two gentlemen within the next half an hour. I'm sure you'll all settle in very easily.' He coughed. 'A word of advice, Mr Johnson. We don't put up with bad behaviour at the Zermatt Academy. I would advise you to stay out of trouble.' Without waiting for a reply, he turned and walked back up the corridor.

Max entered his room. It was small but comfortable. A single bed against one wall, a desk against another and an en-suite shower room. A window looked out onto a snow-covered playing field, with a direct view of the Matterhorn, stark and imposing. He sat on the edge of the bed and remembered the school he had attended back in the days before he had heard

11

of the Special Forces Cadets, before meeting the others. It had been nothing like this. Max had never set foot inside a boarding school before. It felt like a weird mash-up of a country house and a prison.

There was a knock on the door. Max opened it to find a younger man with his suitcase. He indicated that the man should bring the suitcase inside. When he had left, Max started to unpack. He squared away his clothes and put a fake family photograph in a silver frame on his desk. He wanted to go and find Abby and Lili, who had arrived earlier, but that would not be in keeping with their cover story. The cadets were not supposed to know each other. They could 'meet' and make friends once they were here, but it had to look realistic. So, once he had put all his things away, he switched on his laptop, tethered it to his phone and went online. He wanted to check the forecast.

The old man had been right. A heavy band of low pressure was advancing across central Europe. When it hit, it would be bad. He glanced out of the window, up at the mountain range. There would be snowboarders up there, and ski mountaineers traversing the Haute Route between Zermatt and Chamonix. If they had any sense, they'd avoid the slopes when the storm came.

Another knock on the door. Max frowned, then stood up and opened it. Abby and Lili were in the corridor.

'What the . . . ?' Max hissed, angry that they weren't sticking to the script.

'We've got a problem,' Abby interrupted. 'Come on.'

The two girls led Max along the corridor and back out into

the quad. Even before he stepped outside, he could hear a chorus of jeering voices and knew something was happening. As they stepped out into the snow, they could see what. A group of five boys had surrounded a smaller boy. They were laughing at him and pushing him around the circle. Although Max couldn't hear what they were saying, it was clear they were bullying the smaller kid, who was in no state to fight back.

'It's Darius,' Abby whispered. 'Lili met him this morning. He's having a really hard time.' Her eyes narrowed. 'Look at those *idiots*.'

The injustice of what he was seeing made Max's pulse race. He wanted to run across the quad and sort the situation out, single-handed, but something stopped him.

'We wanted to go and deal with them,' Lili said. 'I mean, we *could*, easily. But then we thought, two girls sorting out five boys? Pretty good way to draw attention to ourselves.'

Max nodded his agreement. 'I'm sorry he's having a hard time,' he said. 'But we're here to protect him from worse things than a few school bullies. If we blow our cover, we can't do that.'

As he spoke, the boy Abby had identified as Darius slipped in the snow and fell. There was a loud jeer from the bullies. One of them looked around furtively, clearly checking that there were no adults in the vicinity, then moved closer to Darius and kicked him in the stomach. His friends cheered.

'That's it,' Abby whispered. She looked at Max and Lili. 'To hell with our cover. They can't get away with that.' Without another word, she strode across the quad in the direction of the fight.

Max and Lili looked at each other. 'She's right,' Lili said.

13

Max wrestled with his conscience. 'Come on,' he said. 'We'd better help her.'

They followed Abby across the quad. None of the bullies paid them any attention as they approached. They were too busy laughing at Darius as he squirmed in the snow, clearly in pain. Just as a second bully stepped forward to deliver another kick, Abby cleared her throat noisily. The bully stopped mid-kick. He and his friends turned to look at Abby, and at Max and Lili, who were flanking her.

There was a tense moment of silence, then Abby smiled sweetly. 'Why don't you fellows all trot off back to your rooms?' she said.

One of the bullies stepped forward. He was much taller than any of the cadets, with broad shoulders, floppy brown hair, a sneer and an arrogant swagger. 'Who are you?' he said. 'My mum?'

'I'm very happy to say I'm *not* your mum,' Abby replied. 'I'm not sure I could stand the embarrassment.'

The bully's eyes narrowed. He licked his lips. Max knew what the boy was going to do, even before he did it. But so, clearly, could Abby. As the boy lurched clumsily towards her, she sidestepped. The boy tripped and fell flat on his face in the snow. Quickly he scrambled to his feet, brushing the powder from his clothes.

'Would you like to try that again?' Abby offered. 'It didn't go so well the first time, and I'd hate for you to look silly in front of your little friends.'

Darius had got to his feet and was nervously backing away. The floppy-haired bully was blushing and Max knew, beyond question, that a fight was brewing. As Abby stood over the boy on the ground, Max and Lili stepped forward. Two of the other bullies were already advancing on them. One of them swung a clumsy fist at Max's face. But how was he to know that Max had the advantage of many hours of training in hand-to-hand combat? How was he to know that Max's reactions would be fast and instinctive? Max raised his left elbow to block the punch, then jabbed his free fist into his opponent's solar plexus. Winded, the boy doubled over and staggered back. Max glanced to the left and saw that Lili's guy was already flat on his back. Lili was looking at the guy, her head tipped to one side, as though he was an interesting specimen in a science laboratory. There were two more boys who hadn't yet joined the melee. They looked uncertain. Two of their friends were on the ground, one gasping for breath. They glanced at each other, then around the quad, clearly looking for exit routes.

'What are you doing?' the floppy-haired bully shouted at them. 'Don't just stand there! Do them!'

The two boys exchanged another reluctant glance. In his peripheral vision, Max saw three more people entering the quad: Cavendish the porter, with Lukas and Sami following him. They stopped and looked in the direction of the fight, just as the final two boys hurled themselves at Max and Lili.

In retrospect, Max would have to admit that he hit his guy harder than he had intended. His assailant's forward momentum gave Max's punch more power, and if the boy hadn't slipped in the snow Max's fist would have hit his stomach, not his face. As it was, there was a crack as Max's fist connected with the boy's nose, and blood spattered on the white snow. The bully clutched his nose and started to howl, while Lili's guy received the full force of a sharp kick in the gut and started to gasp for breath. By now, the boys on the ground were back on their feet, but they seemed to have lost their appetite for a fight. As a group, they retreated across the quad, just as Cavendish bellowed, 'What on earth is going on here?'

The porter marched across the snow towards Max, Lili and Abby. He paid no attention to the defeated bullies, but stared furiously at the three cadets as he advanced. Lukas and Sami stood awkwardly where he had left them, maintaining the pretence that they didn't know their friends.

'You haven't even been here a day, and already you're causing trouble!' Cavendish fumed. 'I'll be reporting your behaviour to the headmaster.'

'Will you be reporting theirs?' Abby asked. She pointed at the retreating bullies, and then at Darius, who was cowering in a nearby doorway. 'They were beating him up.'

'Young lady,' said the porter. 'Students who try to take the law into their own hands tend to come a cropper at the Zermatt Academy.' With that, he turned and marched back across the quad.

'That,' Abby muttered, 'could be a problem.'

Max swore under his breath. This was not going well. Their attempt to keep a low profile had already failed. But maybe they could turn the situation to their advantage. Now would be a good time to try to make friends with Darius. Max jogged across the quad to see him.

Darius's eyes were red. He had obviously been crying. As

16

Max approached he seemed to shrink back, like a frightened animal. Max held out his hand. 'Hi there,' he said, trying to sound as friendly as possible. 'I'm Max.' He jabbed a thumb backwards towards the scene of the fight. 'Look, I'm sorry you had to . . .'

He didn't finish his sentence. Shoulders hunched, Darius barged past him. 'Leave me alone,' he said, and he ran across the quad and out of sight.

Max looked back at his friends. Lukas and Sami had joined Abby and Lili. Any pretence that they were strangers had been forgotten.

'What you playing at?' Lukas demanded with a frown as Max walked up to them. 'We're supposed to stay under the radar.'

'Yeah,' Max said. 'Change of plan, I guess. I think I might have broken that guy's nose.' He looked down at the blood-stained snow. 'If someone runs into your fist, what are you supposed to do?'

They stood there in silence for a moment. 'Well,' Abby declared finally, 'I'd say this is all going really well, wouldn't you?' The other cadets glared at her as, somewhere, a bell tolled. 'Lunchtime!' she announced. 'I don't know about you lot, but I get hungry when I've been fighting. I get hungry when I *haven't* been fighting, to be fair. Shall we go? I know where the dining hall is.'

The cadets followed Abby back to the school building. As they walked, something caught Max's eye. He saw a face in a ground-floor window, watching him. It was a craggy face, lined and deeply tanned, with a shock of grey-blond hair and piercing blue eyes. The man was watching Max intently. Their eyes locked for a couple of seconds, then the man stepped back from the window and disappeared.

Max was left with a strange feeling, almost like recognition. But he knew he'd never seen the man before. He was probably just on edge after the fight.

He followed the others back inside.

3

OPSEC

The lunch hall – a vast, oak-panelled room with long tables and two chandeliers hanging from the ceiling – was not busy. Max assumed that most of the students had headed into Zermatt for the day. There was no sign of Darius, or the five bullies. Twenty other students were eating lunch, but they ignored the cadets, who sat together at the end of one table. Max had his phone out and was halfway through a plate of tasty stew when it pinged with a text message from Hector: 'Maison Chocolat, 1500 hours.'

It wasn't an invitation. It was an instruction.

'Looks like I've got an RV with my chaperone,' he said.

Hector, Angel and Woody were staying at a hotel in the centre of Zermatt. Their presence wouldn't attract attention. 'About half the kids at the Academy have their own chaperones,' Hector had explained as they made the journey from the UK to Geneva. 'They're a cross between nannies and bodyguards. If they want to go skiing or go out on an excursion at the weekend, the chaperones accompany them to provide close protection.'

'And to carry the shopping bags,' Angel had added with an arch look.

'For the purposes of this operation, Angel is Abby's chaperone, Woody is Sami's and I'm Max's.'

'Does that mean you have to carry Max's shopping?' Abby asked.

'It means we have cover if we need to make contact. If we do, drop everything to make the RV. Understood?'

Understood. Max shovelled down the rest of his lunch. It was almost 1400 hours already. 'I'll catch you guys later,' he said. 'Try to find Darius, yeah? He needs to be our new best friend.'

Max fetched snow boots, a jacket and sunglasses from his room, then headed across the quad to the exit, which was marked by a stone arch in a high perimeter wall about a football pitch's length from the helipad. In front of the arch was a stone cottage with a brass plaque on the door: 'Porter's Lodge'. As Max approached, he saw Cavendish standing at the window, scowling. But he didn't stop Max from leaving the school grounds, and a minute later Max was striding along the road that led down the hill from the Academy into Zermatt.

The weather had changed. The blue sky had disappeared, snow was falling and the temperature was dropping. Zermatt lay ahead of him, a picturesque collection of snow-topped chalets with steeply pitched roofs. Even though it was only early afternoon, the town was already bathed in a warm yellow light that made the falling snow appear golden. Looking over his shoulder, Max realised he could no longer see the Matterhorn. The cloud was getting lower, the sun only visible as a pale disc.

Zermatt looked inviting; the mountains, threatening. He upped his pace to keep warm.

He knew, from studying a map of the area, that it was just over a kilometre to the centre of Zermatt, but it felt further. There were no cars. The Watchers had explained during their briefing sessions that vehicles were not allowed into Zermatt, with the exception of some electric buses and emergency vehicles such as police cars and fire engines. Tourists were sometimes ferried around by horse-drawn cart. But regular combustion engines were banned, to keep the streets and the mountain air clean.

Max passed groups of what he assumed to be students coming the other way. They glared at him without warmth. He must have been walking for ten minutes when, looking back to check on the visibility of the Matterhorn, he noticed someone following him, just far enough away that Max couldn't see his face. It looked like a man, but that was all Max could say.

When the figure realised that Max had stopped, he stopped too.

Max felt a chill of suspicion. He continued walking a little faster through the outskirts of Zermatt, past a few chalets and shops selling ski gear. After a couple of minutes he looked back again. The figure was still following. Maybe it was nothing to worry about. Maybe it was just some regular guy, walking into town.

Or maybe it wasn't. *Trust nobody*: the Watchers had drilled that into the cadets from day one. Max was on an operation. His situational awareness needed to be second to none.

The road was busier now: there were more shops and cafes

on either side, and crowds of people shuffling through the snow. Two dejected-looking ponies pulled a family in a cart through the snow. The shops were aimed at tourists, selling chocolates and postcards, Swiss Army penknives and snow gear. As the road bent to the left, it was easy for Max to check that he was momentarily out of sight of the man. He found himself next to a little souvenir shop. Its yellow glow spilled invitingly out into the street and its window was crammed with decorative plates and garish paintings of Zermatt. A bell on the door tinkled as he stepped inside, and the warm air was cosseting after the outdoor chill. Nine or ten customers milled around inside the shop, and a little old lady stood behind a counter. None of them paid Max any attention as he stood by the window. He picked up a snow globe with a tiny model of the Matterhorn inside. He shook it, pretending to examine it but really keeping watch on the passers-by.

It took less than a minute for the man to appear. He wore a black North Face jacket with the hood up, black trousers and sturdy shoes. As he passed, Max cursed inwardly. He was unable to ID the man because of his hood.

Suddenly the man stopped. He was almost directly in front of Max, on the other side of the window. Max felt another chill, despite the warmth of the shop. The man was turning to face him.

Their eyes locked.

It was the man who had been watching Max before lunch, through the window looking onto the quad. The same craggy face, the same deep lines and piercing blue eyes. He cocked his head in recognition, gave Max a strange, unsettling smile, then turned and continued on his way.

'*Kann ich ihnen helfen?*' said a voice.

Max turned, aware that he was sweating. The little old lady from behind the counter was standing next to him, meaningfully eyeing the snow globe.

'Um,' Max said. He glanced sideways out of the window. There was no sign of the guy. 'Can you tell me where Maison Chocolat is, please?'

She narrowed her eyes and pointed out of the shop. 'Just across the street,' she said in a Swiss German accent. 'Will you be purchasing that?'

'Maybe another time,' Max said. He replaced the globe, nodded at her and left the shop.

Out in the street, there was no sign of the man in the North Face jacket. Max cursed himself. If the Watchers knew how he'd been tracked just then, they'd have something to say about it. He looked across the street, saw Maison Chocolat and hurried across to it. It looked invitingly warm inside. The front window was misted up and a delicious aroma of coffee wafted out into the street. Max entered and looked around.

He saw Hector immediately: he knew he would have his back to the far wall so that he had eyes on the exit. But what Max hadn't expected was to see the man with the North Face jacket sitting at the same table. He no longer had his hood up, so his shock of grey-blond hair was visible. And although he didn't have Hector's full beard, even though he didn't particularly *look* like Hector, now they were side by side there was something undeniably similar about the two men. Maybe it was their broad shoulders. Maybe it was their square jaw. Maybe it was the strong stare they gave him as he approached their table.

'Want to tell me what's going on?' Max said.

Coffee cups chinked all around him. There was a low hubbub of conversation. If anybody was paying attention to this uncomfortable meeting, they didn't show it. Hector made a hand gesture to indicate that Max should sit, which he did.

'It could be him,' said the stranger. 'I feel like I've gone back in time fifteen years.'

'Why were you following me?' Max said. But before the man could answer, a waiter arrived. Max ordered a hot chocolate, then turned back to Hector. 'What's going on?' he repeated.

'Max, I want you to meet Alfie Grey. Former 22 SAS, Mountain Troop. Probably the best Alpine guide in the world.'

'That still doesn't explain why he was following me.'

'Same way of talking,' said Alfie Grey. 'Blunt.'

'Alfie knew your dad,' Hector said quietly. He took a sip of his coffee while the information sank in.

'Right,' Max said quietly.

'Knew him,' Alfie Grey said, 'fought alongside him, and liked him. Very much. He was a good man, Max. One of the best.'

Max found himself frowning and realised he was trying to hold back tears. He said nothing.

'I only found out this morning that Alfie's now a teacher at the Zermatt Academy. Cushy job – teaching rich kids how to snowboard. I knew there was a good chance your paths would cross, and an even better chance that he would recognise you. Better to have this out in the open.'

'What about operational security?' Max said.

Alfie smiled. 'Truly Reg Johnson's son, worrying about OPSEC,' he said. The waiter arrived with Max's hot chocolate.

24

They were silent as he placed it on the table then withdrew. 'There was always a rumour,' Alfie said, 'that Reg had a little side project. A team of . . . kids, I guess you'd call them. I thought it was just Regiment gossip. Never really believed it.' He took a sip of his coffee, eyeing Max over the cup. Max glanced at Hector, unsure what to say. They remained silent. Alfie replaced his coffee cup. 'Don't worry, lads,' he said. 'I'm not expecting you to confirm or deny anything. Just know this: if you need help – help of any kind – you only have to ask. A friend of Reg's is a friend of mine. And a *son* of Reg's? Let's just say, I've got your back.' Alfie stood up, shook Hector's hand, then Max's. 'Nice work in the quad this afternoon, by the way,' he said. 'I've been wanting to do the same to that little group of idiots for ages now, but apparently it's not the done thing for teachers to break students' noses.'

Max flushed.

'Don't worry, son,' said Alfie. 'I'll sort it out with the school. We won't be expelling you just yet.' He winked at Max, then left the cafe.

'Broken nose?' Hector said as they watched him leave.

'Yeah,' Max replied. 'He kind of fell on my fist.'

'You're supposed to be keeping a low profile.'

'Right. It, er, it didn't quite work out like that.'

'*Make it* work out like that.'

Max wanted to change the subject. 'Does he know why we're here? Alfie Grey, I mean.'

Hector shook his head. 'No. But he's not stupid. He knows you're undercover. He's a good man. A brave soldier. He'll help you if you ask him.' Hector peered over at the exit. 'You

25

should be getting back. The weather's getting worse. A storm's coming in.'

'Yeah, I heard.'

'It wouldn't surprise me if they closed the lifts and started to bring people back down from the mountain.' He gave Max a piercing stare. 'Look after that kid, Max. You wouldn't want to be in his shoes if the Iranians got their hands on him. Anything suspicious, report back to me. I only need the slightest excuse to get him and the rest of you airlifted out of there.'

'Roger that,' Max said. Leaving his hot chocolate untouched, he stood up and left the cafe.

The snow was falling even more heavily outside. Max strode back past the souvenir shops to the outskirts of the town and headed through the blizzard to the school, snow settling on his clothes as he walked.

4

Room 23

It was mathematics that did it.

When Max returned to the school, shivering and covered with snow, he felt the need for company. The conversation about his father had unsettled him. His relationship with his dead parents – or, rather, his lack of it – was deeply personal. He didn't know how he felt about meeting one of his dad's old friends, someone who had known him well. He couldn't shake the idea that Alfie Grey was intruding somehow. So, after going back to his room and getting out of his snow gear, he went to find the others.

He found Lili in the library. It was a vast, dark, musty room with bookshelves twice the height of a man, and ladders on wheels to reach the upper shelves. Lili was sitting at a desk in the middle of the room, books open in front of her. Darius was by her side, similarly engrossed. Apart from Max, they were the only people in the library.

'Hey,' he said, walking over to them.

They looked up from their books. 'Hey,' Lili said with a half-smile.

Darius remained silent. He didn't seem to want to catch Max's eye. Maybe he was embarrassed about earlier on. Max offered him his hand. 'I'm Max,' he said. 'I'm new here. Look, I'm sorry about earlier. I just thought maybe you could use some help.' He grinned. 'You might have to return the favour if I bump into those boys any time soon.'

Max's light-hearted comment didn't hit the mark. Darius frowned and turned back to his books.

'We're doing calculus,' Lili said.

'Right,' Max said. 'Er, what's that?'

Darius looked up again. 'It's about continuous rates of change,' he said. His voice was deep and his English was good. 'Lili and I were trying to work out how to integrate this function.' He pointed at some symbols on the page that meant nothing to Max.

'I think I've got it,' said Lili. She showed him her working, and Darius's face lit up. They bumped fists, and it was clear that they'd bonded.

Yeah, Max thought with a smile, it was the mathematics that had done it. Nicely played, Lili.

'Maybe we should call it a day,' Lili said. 'I'm getting hungry . . .'

'Who's that?' Max whispered. He'd heard a movement behind a nearby bookcase that jutted out at right angles to the wall. He and Lili exchanged a worried glance. Max made a 'stay there' gesture, then walked quietly towards the bookcase. The noise had stopped. He felt a chill, like a draught, and found himself clenching his fists as he moved stealthily around the end of the bookcase to see who was there.

Nobody. There was a door leading out of the library, which was ajar. That was where the draught came from. Maybe he'd just heard it banging.

He was turning back to rejoin the others when he noticed something else. A little lump of snow lay on the ground, melting onto the wooden floorboards. Someone *had* been here. Max thought about following and trying to find them, but decided against it. It wasn't as if the library was out of bounds. He returned to Lili and Darius.

'Just a door banging,' he said.

'There's a storm coming,' said Darius. 'At least that's what they say.' He started to pack up his books.

And suddenly they were all friends. Max and Lili accompanied Darius to the dining hall that evening. They sat with the other cadets and bonded over plates of tartiflette oozing with melted cheese, which Abby gobbled down and Lukas looked at like it was poison. When the bullies entered, Darius seemed relieved to have some friends around him. The ringleader with the floppy hair gave them an aggressive look, but he and his mates kept their distance. After dinner, they watched TV in a day room with comfortable sofas and a 40-inch screen. A few other students poked their head around the door, but when they saw who was in there they opted not to join them. It was obvious that everyone had decided the cadets and Darius were to be avoided. At ten o'clock, Darius announced he was going to bed.

'More calculus tomorrow?' Lili suggested.

Darius grinned in reply and left the room.

Now the cadets were alone, they could talk. 'What did Hector want?' Sami asked earnestly.

'Nothing, really,' Max said. He felt bad about lying to his friends, but he didn't feel like discussing Alfie Grey and his parents. 'Just touching base, you know?'

'You don't think those bullies were anything to do with the Iranians?' said Abby.

'I don't think so,' Max said. 'Professional kidnappers – assassins – are going to be more skilful and dangerous than those jokers.'

'That's what I thought.' Abby nodded thoughtfully.

'We should watch his room,' Lukas said. 'At night, I mean. If we were going to kidnap him, that's when we'd do it, right?'

The cadets nodded.

'He's in our corridor,' Lili said. 'Room 23. We can hide in one of the alcoves near his room, under all the snow gear. Do it in shifts, ninety minutes each. I'll go first if you like. Max, I'll knock on your door at midnight. Then Lukas, then Sami, then Abby?'

More nods. The cadets returned to their rooms. Lili lingered in the corridor outside, pretending to be playing with her phone. A stillness fell over the school. In his room, Max looked out of the window. Snow was falling so thickly that he could barely see a couple of metres, even with his room light off. It felt like the snow was muffling everything, closing in on them. It was unnaturally quiet. It made Max feel uneasy.

He lay on his bed, knowing he should sleep. But sleep didn't come, and soon there was a gentle tap on his door. He got up and stepped out into the corridor. Nobody was there. Not even Lili. He closed his door quietly behind him and strode up the corridor – it was dim, lit only by tiny security lights in the ceiling – to the alcove opposite, just beyond Room 23. It was stuffed with piles of ski jackets and salopettes. Max wormed his way into the corner, covered himself with the clothing, leaving just a crack for his eyes, and waited.

His mind was turning over. On previous operations they'd had a specific objective. A task. This was different. They didn't know for sure if anybody was coming for Darius. They didn't know who to look out for, when it would happen, or how. Somehow, that made it worse. There was a gnawing anxiety in the pit of his stomach. It was like watching a scary movie, and waiting for the jump.

He'd been under the coats for about half an hour when he heard a noise. Footsteps at one end of the corridor, and the hiss of whispers. He held his breath, crouching statue-still in his hiding place as the footsteps approached. His thoughts raced. It must be midnight. Who was walking down the corridor at this time? Was someone coming for Darius? He glanced at the opposite wall and saw a fire-alarm button behind a glass panel. If he had to, he could activate it to alert people . . .

Five figures came into view. Max recognised them immediately. The bullies were no longer dressed in their outdoor gear, of course, but in pyjamas and dressing gowns. They congregated outside Darius's door, whispering to each other, clearly planning to do something unpleasant.

Max didn't know what to do. Should he stand up to these boys again and reveal his hiding place in the process? That would draw even more attention to himself. And anyway, could he deal with all five boys himself?

Did he have a choice?

They were crowding around Darius's door now, getting ready to barge in. Had Darius locked it from the inside? Would they break the door down? What was their problem with the Iranian boy anyway?

Max felt his muscles clenching. He knew he had to do something. It was like he was hardwired not to let these idiots have their way. He prepared to throw off the ski jackets and stand up to the bullies for the second time that day.

'What's going on here?'

The voice came from the opposite end of the corridor. Max recognised it immediately. Alfie Grey. He kept perfectly still and waited.

The bullies turned to look at the teacher. They had a look on their faces that Max recognised from his own days at school: the sneering expression of a pupil who has no respect for the teachers, and who isn't about to be talked down to. The floppy-haired ringleader stood in front of the others as Mr Grey approached.

'Couldn't sleep, sir,' he said, his voice dripping with contempt.

Mr Grey was standing in front of them now. Max couldn't see his face, but he towered above the five students. 'I suggest you try a bit harder,' he growled.

'Don't think we will, actually, sir,' said the ringleader. 'And since our parents pay your wages, maybe you shouldn't speak to us like that?'

Silence, broken only by a snort of laughter from one of the other boys.

When it happened, it happened quickly. Mr Grey grabbed the ringleader by the front of his dressing gown with one hand, swung him around and pinned him against the wall. Alarmed, the others took a step back.

'Listen to me, sunshine,' said Mr Grey, his voice quiet but every word very clear. 'You made a fool of yourself in the quad earlier on and you're making a fool of yourself now. You might find it amusing to talk to your other teachers like that, but understand this: I've gone eyeball to eyeball with the Taliban in Afghanistan. You think a handful of spoiled rich kids worry me? If I find you bullying Darius or anyone again, I'll break every bone in your body. And you can tell your billionaire daddy I said so.'

He let the ringleader go. The boy staggered back to where his mates were standing. His face was a picture of outrage, but he was plainly too scared to say anything. He made a shooing gesture at the others and they quickly shuffled out of sight.

Mr Grey stood in the dim corridor watching them go. Max's heart was thumping hard. Mr Grey didn't move at first. Only when the bullies had disappeared did he turn. His head was cocked. One eyebrow was raised. His lined, craggy face looked half suspicious, half amused – as though he thought he was being watched. His gaze fell momentarily on the alcove and for a few seconds he was looking directly at Max's position. He smiled knowingly, then his gaze moved on. Thirty seconds later, he had disappeared.

Max was sweating with relief that he hadn't been seen. Or had he? Had Mr Grey known he was hiding there? Had he left him alone because he understood, after the meeting with Hector, that Max and the others were not at the Zermatt Academy to learn, but for some other reason?

The rest of his watch passed without incident. At 0100 hours he climbed out from under the ski jackets and knocked on Lukas's door. His friend appeared, bleary eyed. 'Anything?' he muttered.

'The bullies,' Max said.

Lukas's eyes narrowed with aggression.

'It's okay,' Max said. 'I don't think they'll be back. I'll explain in the morning. Just stay hidden.'

With that, he returned to his room, where he undressed, climbed into bed and fell into a disturbed sleep.

5

Thundersnow

Max was woken by a knock on the door. He opened it groggily to find Abby standing there, dressed.

'Breakfast?' she said. 'The others are ready.'

'And Darius?'

'He's with Lili. They're talking maths again.' A pained look crossed her face. 'I love Lili like a sister, but I wish she'd change the subject.'

'Nah, it's good,' said Max. 'It keeps Darius close. Give me two minutes.'

Quickly, Max dressed. He and Abby joined the others in the dining hall, where they sat over toast and tea with Darius. The Iranian boy was talking animatedly with Lili, while Lukas and Sami appeared somewhat stunned by the conversation. It looked like they weren't into calculus either. There were maybe thirty other students milling around, but no sign of the bullies. Five teachers sat at the head table, including Cavendish and Mr Grey, who paid no attention to Max. Max and Abby grabbed some cereal and went to sit with the others. They'd managed to move Darius and Lili on from maths, and were discussing how they might spend their Sunday.

'We could go skiing!' Sami said, his voice full of enthusiasm.

Darius shook his head. 'I don't really like the snow.'

'You've come to the wrong place,' Lukas said.

'Yes, well, my father . . .' Darius frowned. 'Never mind. Can't we just go to the library? I have some studying to do.'

'Sure,' said Lili. 'I'll come with you.'

And that was that. After breakfast, Lili accompanied Darius to the library while the others walked around the school and its grounds. To any casual observer, they were four new arrivals checking out the Academy. In reality, they were committing the layout of the building and its grounds to memory. They had examined satellite images of the school, but that was no substitute for a proper recce.

It wasn't easy. Thick snow was still falling from a grey sky. Visibility was only a few metres. The turrets of the school were mere shadows behind them, and there was no sign of the surrounding mountains.

'We can't just leave him to Lili,' Sami said as they walked around a snow-covered rugby pitch towards the perimeter fence that surrounded the grounds. Max didn't like leaving footsteps in the snow, but he had no option if they wanted to check the fence for weak spots by which enemy personnel might enter – or through which the cadets might leave in an emergency. Anyway, the heavy snowfall would re-cover them quickly.

'I agree,' said Abby. 'Our orders are not to leave him alone at any point, so we each have to find something in common with him somehow.'

'As long as I don't have to talk about maths,' Lukas muttered.

'I don't think it'll be too hard,' Max said. 'Not once Lili's broken the ice. He's obviously not very popular. He'll be glad of some friends.'

The others nodded their agreement and continued to walk.

It took a couple of hours to cover the perimeter. It was completely secure. Shivering, they returned to the school buildings and put on dry clothes. Abby, Sami and Lukas went to find lunch. Max headed to the library. He was still wearing a coat and gloves, as he knew how chilly it was in there, and sturdy boots to protect his feet from the snow. Darius and Lili were at their table, warmly dressed, and even Lili looked a little wild-eyed at the textbooks sprawled out in front of them.

'Hey, Lili,' Max said. 'Abby was looking for you.'

Lili gave him a grateful look, then turned to Darius. 'I'd better go find her,' she said.

A flicker of disappointment crossed Darius's face as she stood up and left. 'I could help you carry these books back,' Max said.

'No,' Darius replied. 'I should carry on working.'

'Mate, you've got to relax sometimes, hey? Why don't we hang out for a bit?'

Darius hesitated before reluctantly nodding.

'Cool,' Max said with an enthusiasm he didn't really feel. 'Come on, then.' He started to collect up the books while Darius put his own coat and gloves on. A few seconds later, he and Darius had armfuls of books. 'Shall we take these back

37

to your room?' Max said. Darius nodded wordlessly, and it occurred to Max that keeping a conversation going with this guy was going to be hard work. 'It's still snowing,' he said as they left the library. 'Feels like it's never going to stop.'

'I'm used to a hot country,' Darius said. 'Iran.' He frowned. 'But I can't go back there.'

They left the library and emerged into a cloistered walkway that stretched along one side of the quad. To their ten o'clock was the area where the bullies had beaten Darius up. To their three o'clock was the door that led to their bedrooms. They could barely see the far side of the quad for snow, which lay two feet deep on the ground. Max hunched his shoulders, ready to battle across the quad through the elements. 'Let's do it,' he said. He stepped out into the quad, his feet crunching in the snow, Darius trailing behind him.

If Max hadn't heard the call of a bird, at least one of them would have been dead. It sounded like a crow, but it was so loud and unusual, ringing out above the silent quad, that Max stopped to look up for it.

As he looked up, he saw the figure.

It was just an outline, indistinguishable through the blizzard, its upper half visible above the ancient pitched roof to Max's right. Although he couldn't see the face, he could tell from the hunched shape that it was a gunman, weapon engaged, ready to fire.

Max's reflexes were like lightning. He dropped the maths books, spun around and threw himself at Darius, who cried out in surprise as Max tackled him to the ground. Out of the corner of his eye, Max saw a red dot flickering on the snow to his left. He rolled away from it just as he heard the distant retort of a suppressed weapon – and a screech and flapping of wings as the unseen bird lifted into the sky. A bullet exploded in the snow no more than an arm's length from him.

'*Run!*' he barked, pushing himself to his feet and grabbing Darius. Darius's books were all over the place and he didn't look scared, but outraged.

'Come on!'

The red dot danced nearby again, approaching along the snow. As Darius scrambled to his feet, Max dragged him ferociously back towards the cloistered walkway. There was an explosion of masonry as the bullet hit one of the fluted columns and ricocheted to the ground. By that time, Max and Darius were sprinting along the walkway back to the library. They burst through the door, breathless.

'What's happening?' Darius said.

Max looked around the room. The only other exit was the one Max had found the previous day. Should they go through it, or would they find another gunman?

'What's happening?' Darius repeated.

'*Quiet!*' Max hissed. There were footsteps coming from the direction of the cloistered walkway. Somebody was running towards them. Max grabbed Darius by the wrist and pulled him towards the other exit. 'We need to get out of here . . .' he hissed as they picked up speed.

'Max!' The voice was strong and authoritative. Max looked back. It was Mr Grey. He had burst into the library. 'Are you okay? I heard gunshots.' His voice was no-nonsense.

Max felt a wave of relief. 'There's a shooter,' he said. 'On the roof. He tried to get Darius. Nearly got me.'

Mr Grey's eyes narrowed, as if he took an attempt on Max's life as a personal insult. 'We need to get you out of here,' he said. 'Do you have your phone?'

Max nodded and pulled his phone from his pocket.

'Call Hector. Do it now.'

'Tell me what's going on!' Darius shouted.

Mr Grey strode up to him, his face like a thundercloud. 'Do you want to stay alive?' he demanded.

Darius blinked, then nodded.

'Then you do *exactly* what *I* say and what *he* says.' He pointed at Max, who had already dialled Hector and had his phone to his ear.

Hector answered immediately.

Go ahead.

'Someone just shot at me and Darius from the rooftop.'

Are you hurt?

'No.'

Where are you?

'In the library. Mr Grey's with us.'

A pause.

You need to get out of the school. All of you, Darius included. It's not safe. Get into Zermatt. We'll get you all out of here. Mission over. I'll call the others. You concentrate on evacuating Darius. Put me on to Alfie.

Max didn't reply. He handed his phone to Mr Grey, who listened to Hector for thirty seconds before replying. 'Understood.' He hung up and handed the phone back. 'I'm going to escort you to the exit. Once we're there, I'm going to keep the cordon in place. Nobody will enter or leave without my permission. You'll RV at Maison Chocolat. Follow me!'

Mr Grey led them back out to the walkway. 'Where was the shooter?' he asked Max, who pointed to the roof. Word had clearly spread that something had happened. Despite the snow, there were maybe twenty people in the quad, calling to each other. Mr Grey pointed across the quad to the arch that led to the exit. 'Let's go,' he said. 'Whoever it was won't risk still being there. I'll stand on your right, to be safe. *Move!*'

So, with Mr Grey shielding them, Max and Darius sprinted across the quad. A couple of boys shouted, 'Hey, sir, what's happening?'

Mr Grey ignored them. He seemed completely focused on getting Max and Darius out of there. A minute later they had cleared the quad and were sprinting through the blizzard, past the helipad towards the porter's lodge. As they approached, Cavendish emerged. 'No exeats now,' he announced. 'The weather's too bad.'

'It's okay, Mike,' said Mr Grey. 'They have my permission.'

Cavendish frowned, but stepped aside and let them pass.

'Maison Chocolat,' Mr Grey reminded them. 'I'll send the others there. Don't move till you hear from Hector.'

Max nodded. He turned to Darius. 'You have to trust us,' he said.

Darius swallowed hard and nodded. Together, they ran.

Max was thankful that they were dressed in their snow gear. They almost overheated as they ran. After a couple of minutes Max heard sirens and two police cars came into view, their snow chains crunching, windscreen wipers flapping, headlights burning through the blizzard. Max couldn't see who was in them. Regular police? The Watchers? He kept Darius close as they passed on their way to the school. Their sirens quickly faded and became muffled. But then there was a flash of lightning. It lit up the entire sky: for a split second Max, could see the jagged, ghostly shapes of the mountains surrounding Zermatt. Moments later, there was a crack of thunder. It rolled and echoed around the mountains.

'Thundersnow,' Max shouted at Darius. 'It's pretty rare. That's a bad storm above us.'

Darius didn't reply. They kept running.

The streets of Zermatt were less busy than yesterday. Any pedestrians were either hurrying into shops and cafes or standing in huddled groups looking up at the sky. They ignored Max and Darius, who ran past the souvenir shop towards Maison Chocolat. Before they reached it, however, Max suddenly stopped, grabbing Darius and forcing him to a halt.

'What is it?' Darius hissed.

Max didn't reply immediately. He was too focused on what he had seen: a figure standing in a doorway opposite Maison Chocolat. He was not gazing in wonder at the storm, or hurrying from the elements. He was watching the entrance to the cafe. Max didn't like it. He looked over his shoulder. To his relief, the other cadets were just visible. Lili was on the same side of the street, outside the souvenir shop. Abby and Lukas were a little further back on the opposite pavement. Several metres behind them was Lukas. They were all watching Max and Darius.

'You see Lili?' Max said.

Darius nodded.

'Walk back to her now. Stick with her. Do whatever she says. Understood?'

'I wish you would tell me what was happening.'

'I will. But right now, we need to stay safe. *Go!*'

Darius did as he was told. Max waited until he had reached Lili before striding towards Maison Chocolat, making eye contact with the guy watching. The man frowned, then narrowed his eyes. He clearly knew he had been made. He looked left and right, as though wondering what to do. Max crossed his arms, making it clear that he intended to mark him, because that meant one less person threatening Darius.

He glanced to his left. Lili was hustling Darius back up the street. Another flash of lightning lit up the snow, and a boom echoed around the mountains. Lili and Darius vanished.

6

Lightning

Anxiety gnawed at Lili's stomach.

She didn't know why Max had sent Darius back to her, but there had to be a reason. Mr Grey, urging them out of the school grounds, had told them to RV at the Maison Chocolat cafe, but for some reason Max didn't want them to enter. So she grabbed Darius by the wrist and walked him in the opposite direction as the storm rolled overhead. She'd never seen lightning in the snow before, and it scared her.

Where to go? She had no idea. It occurred to her to duck into a shop or cafe, but if there was a threat, that would restrict her exit strategies. It was better, she decided, to stay out in the open – at least until she knew what was going on. She linked arms with Darius and led him back up the way they'd come before taking a left turn up an almost identical road. There were cute chalet-style buildings on either side, and shops. Lili and Darius strode past them.

'I don't get it,' Darius said breathlessly. 'Why would someone try to shoot Max?'

Lili stopped and looked at him. 'Darius, it was *you* they were trying to shoot.'

He blinked at her.

'Because of your dad.'

'How do you know about my dad?' Darius said. 'That's a secret.'

'Nothing's a secret. Not completely. We're here to watch over you, in case something happens. Well, guess what: it just did, and we have to get you out of here.' She looked over her shoulder. The snow was falling so thickly now that she couldn't see the junction where they'd just turned, or the other cadets. Had they lost each other? She didn't know. But two broad-shouldered men were advancing towards them. They wore heavy black coats dusted with snow. One of them had his hand in his pocket. It looked to Lili as if he was reaching for a handgun. Bile rose in her throat. '*Run!*' she hissed.

Darius didn't need telling twice. They sprinted up the road. As they ran, Lili looked back again. The two men were following. They weren't running, but they were striding with purpose. Their grim faces made Lili feel sick. She knew they would fire if she let them get close enough. Darius slipped and stumbled in the snow. Lili had to grip his arm hard to keep him upright. When she looked back again, the two men were closer.

Where were the others? How had she lost them?

Nobody else was paying them any attention. They were too busy hurrying inside or wondering at the storm. Lili was frustrated at being unable to run as fast as she wanted. The snow held her back, and so did Darius.

The two men were gaining on her.

And then, up ahead, glowing through the blizzard, she saw the flashing lights of a police car.

The siren was not blaring. At first, Lili couldn't tell which direction it was facing. As they stumbled closer, however, they saw that it was facing away from them. The car's rear windscreen wiper was swishing, and fumes billowed from the exhaust pipe. The engine was turning over. Lili urged Darius to up their pace towards the police car. Another glance over her shoulder told her that the two men were holding back a little. Lili practically hurled herself at the car and thumped on the driver's window. As she did so, another blistering flash of lightning lit up the mountains. She was momentarily aware of the craggy shape of the Matterhorn towering over them, but it disappeared as the lightning subsided. Now she was face to face with a Swiss police officer, who had rolled down his window.

'*Ja?*' he asked.

Lili knew enough German to reply. '*Zwei Männer verfolgen uns! Hilfe!*' Two men are chasing us! Help!

The police officer looked bemused. He gestured to the back seat, indicating that they should get inside.

Sweating heavily despite the snow, Lili opened the back seat and urged Darius to get into the car before climbing in after him. She felt a surge of relief as the door slammed shut and the driver activated the central locking. She twisted around and looked through the back window. The two men were still there, standing in the middle of the road, side by side. The gun guy no longer seemed to be reaching for his weapon. Their expressions were cold and hard. Lili suppressed an urge to point the men out. It would only delay them. The important thing was to get away from them, and they surely wouldn't risk messing with the police officers.

Slowly, the police car pulled away, its snow chains crunching, neon lights flashing in the blizzard. The driver flicked a switch on the dashboard and the siren started.

'Where are we going?' Darius said.

'Somewhere safe, I hope,' Lili replied.

Max was shivering. Standing still had made his body temperature drop. But he had no plans to move. The guy in the doorway opposite was still in position. Their gazes were still locked. So long as he stayed there, it meant that Darius had one less guy after him. Max tried to work out what the man's appearance said about him. He was broad shouldered. His nose had once been broken. Max figured it hadn't happened in a skiing accident. He looked like a rough guy on rough business. Max's gut told him that these were men hired by the Iranians to assassinate Darius, and he felt his lip curl at the thought.

Somewhere, not far away, he heard a police siren. He pulled out his phone and dialled Abby. She answered immediately.

'What's happening?' he said.

Lili and Darius just got into a police car.

'Good idea.'

Yeah, I think a couple of guys were after them.

'Can you see these guys?'

Yeah. They're pretty ugly.

'Follow them.'

Roger that.

He hung up. Maybe he should call Lili, but he didn't want to distract her from whatever she was doing. He pocketed his phone again and, as he did so, he noticed something strange. The guy in the doorway wasn't looking at him any more. He was looking to his left, at a figure approaching through the snow.

It was a police officer. He wore a hi-vis snow jacket and he was walking up to the guy in the doorway. He nodded, then turned and walked away again. The guy in the doorway looked over at Max, a malicious grin crossing his face.

Max felt lead in his stomach. He knew what this meant. Either the assassins had infiltrated the Zermatt police force, or they were impersonating the police in order to get close to Darius. He sprinted back the way he'd come, pulling his phone from his pocket and dialling Lili's number as he ran.

The police car continued to crunch through the snow. Lili couldn't see the two men any more. They turned off the main road and onto a side street where there were very few pedestrians.

'*Wohin reisen wir?*' Lili asked. Where are we going?

There was no reply. The driver glanced at Lili in the rear-view mirror. Something in his expression chilled her.

'Stop the car,' she whispered.

No reply.

She tried to open the door. Locked.

'*Stop the car!*' She rattled the door handle and with her other hand undid her seat belt.

No reply.

Her phone vibrated in her pocket. She reached for it. Only then did the police officer in the passenger seat turn. He held a handgun, and pointed it directly at Lili.

'Don't answer it,' he said in perfect, unaccented English.

Lili raised her hands to show that she was obeying. She didn't move her gaze from the weapon, but could sense Darius trembling in the seat next to her. The vehicle accelerated. Its siren was still blaring and Lili was aware of the neon lights illuminating the snow all around them.

'You're not really police officers, are you?' she said.

The gunman didn't answer. His face was expressionless as he kept the pistol pointed at her.

'You should know,' Lili said, 'that we're not alone. We have back-up. Our friends are right behind us.'

'In that case,' said the gunman, 'maybe we should just kill you both right now.'

Lili felt the muscles in her face tensing up. She evaluated her options. The weapon was approximately thirty centimetres from her face. The gunman would surely be underestimating her. She could grab the gun in less than a second and nudge his arm away so that she was no longer in the line of fire. It would cause confusion – and she could use that confusion to gain the upper hand.

No. It wasn't an option. The weapon was cocked and the gunman's finger was resting on the trigger. He might release a round, on purpose or by accident. Even if the bullet missed Lili and Darius, it could ricochet in the enclosed space.

Right now, there was nothing she could do.

Her phone buzzed again. She let it ring. It fell silent.

She glanced out of the window. They were on a deserted road, beyond the boundaries of Zermatt. No houses, no shops. Trees heavy with snow. The mountainside sloped upwards on their right. She looked in the rear-view mirror again, trying to see the road behind them, desperately hoping that she might catch a glimpse of one of the others, following them.

There was nothing.

'Where are we going?' Darius said. Her voice was trembling.

No answer. The driver turned off the siren and the neon light. They drove on.

Max tore up the street, panic burning in his chest, his phone pressed to his ear as Lili failed to answer for a second time. He found Sami waiting for them at a corner.

'We lost them!' Sami said. 'They ran ahead and got into a police car. The others are following, but they're on foot.' He raised his hands as if to indicate that pursuit was hopeless.

'It's not a real police car,' Max said, catching his breath.

'What do you mean?'

'Just trust me. They've been taken. We have to help them. *Come on!*'

They ran together. Thunder roared above them and the snow danced and swirled dramatically, compromising their vision as heavy flakes flew into their eyes. Max wished he could run faster, but the snow slowed him down and he had to work hard not to slip. He could still faintly hear the siren. He and Sami followed it. In a few minutes they were on a road leading out of Zermatt. They passed a sign showing a picture of a chair lift, snow settling thickly on its upper edge. From time to time he could see two grey figures up ahead. He hoped that was Abby and Lukas, also giving chase. He pulled his phone out to make contact with them, but as he did so there was a roll of thunder overhead – louder than any they'd heard so far. The whole sky crackled with lightning. Max could feel the electricity in the air. Sami grabbed Max by the arm and pulled him to a halt.

There was an enormous crash up ahead. Something was happening . . .

The thunder was so loud, Lili could almost feel the car vibrating.

But that was nothing compared to what followed.

A fork of lightning stretched from the sky to the ground. Lili gasped with shock. She could almost taste the electric charge in the air, and its brightness dazzled her momentarily. Was it going to hit the car? She lowered her head and covered it with her arms. Then she heard a massive crack. She looked up. The gunman had lowered his weapon and was looking forward. Up ahead, on the left-hand side of the road, a burning tree was falling. The driver hit the brakes and twisted the steering wheel, but he was losing control and the car was skidding towards the burning tree . . .

When the tree hit the front of the car, Lili thought it was the end. The vehicle jolted violently. The bonnet crumpled as if it was made of paper. The windscreen cracked and a thick, acrid cloud of smoke billowed into the car. Lili's face slammed against the seat in front of her. She felt blood trickle from her nostrils and there was a ringing in her ears. Dizziness and nausea threatened to overcome her. She inhaled deeply, coughed and tried to focus.

The two fake police officers were slumped over the dashboard. The bonnet was burning. Darius seemed unhurt but was staring, looking shocked, into the middle distance. Lili threw herself forward, eyes watering, lungs heaving, and reached over to the dashboard, where she flicked the central locking switch. Amazingly, the car's electrics were still operational. The locks clunked open. Lili pushed open her door and pulled the stunned Darius out into the snow. They staggered away from the smoking vehicle and blazing tree, which completely blocked the road.

They were just in time. There was a brutal explosion as the police car's fuel tank ignited. Lili and Darius threw themselves into the fast-melting snow at the edge of the road. Looking back, Lili saw the car engulfed in black smoke. For a moment, it occurred to her that she should run back and attempt to rescue the two men, despite everything. Then there was a second explosion, deep orange in the heart of the smoke, and she knew it was hopeless. They had to be dead.

Lili and Darius were cough-retching from the smoke. Lili didn't notice Lukas and Abby until they were almost upon her. They were breathless, their faces pinched and their heads and clothes covered in snow.

'What the hell happened?' Abby shouted above the roar of the flames.

'We thought they were police,' Lili spluttered. 'They kidnapped us! Where are Max and Sami?'

'I'll call them,' said Lukas. He pulled out his phone, then

swore. 'No service,' he said. 'Maybe the storm's taken out the communications masts.'

'We need to get away from here,' Abby said. 'This place is going to be swarming with people before we know it.' As she spoke, they saw two more figures approaching through the snow. 'Max!' Abby said, the relief in her voice obvious. 'Sami!'

The boys took in the situation with one sweeping glance. Max pointed at the car. 'Are they dead?'

Lili nodded mutely.

'There's at least two other guys out there,' Max said. 'One of them was watching the cafe. Another was dressed as a policeman. We need to call the Watchers to warn them.'

'Phones are down,' Lukas replied. He frowned as Max verified this on his own handset.

'Probably . . .'

'. . . the storm,' Lukas completed his sentence. 'What should we do?'

'I vote we get back into town,' Lili said. 'It'll be harder for anyone to hurt us when there's more people around.'

'They just made a pretty good stab at it,' Abby said.

'Yeah, well, this time we'll avoid the police . . .'

'*GET DOWN!*' Max shouted.

The cadets hit the ground, Lili bringing Darius down with them. And just in time. A bullet pinged over them from the direction of the town. It flew harmlessly into the burning tree. When she looked back, Lili could just make out three grey figures in the blizzard, one of them with a weapon raised.

'Run!' she said.

The cadets needed no persuasion. They staggered towards

53

the burning tree. The heat was fierce. It melted the snow for several metres on either side. It was just possible, however, to squeeze between the fallen tree and the upward slope of the mountainside. The cadets passed the conflagration in single file and continued to sprint along the road.

Lili was the last to pass the tree. As she ran, she looked back. Through the flames, she could just make out two figures, distorted and hazy, chasing them.

She turned again, and ran.

7

Chair Lift

There had been many times on previous operations when Max had been glad of the gruelling training programmes the Watchers had put them through back at Valley House. While the cadets were being forced to run up and down the bleak Scottish slopes of the place they had learned to call home, they had hated it. But now Max was thankful for his body's strength and speed.

The snow was both a menace and a blessing. It slowed them as they ran, but the blizzard was thick enough to hide them from the gunmen. So for now, there were no more bullets.

Darius did not have the cadets' level of fitness. They took it in turns to practically drag him through the snow. He was panicked and tearful. Max didn't blame him. He remembered how shocked he'd been when he was shot at for the first time. It wasn't a feeling you easily forgot. Now wasn't the time to mollycoddle Darius, however. Their lives depended on Darius keeping up with them, so they barked urgent encouragement at him every few steps.

They were running blind, with no idea of where the road headed. Hiding wasn't an option, because their footprints in the snow would lead the gunmen directly to them. All they could do was forge onwards and hope that an opportunity presented itself. Max remembered passing a ski-lift sign. Maybe there would be crowds – and safety.

It was hard to tell how far they'd run, because the blizzard made everything look the same. A kilometre? Two? Whatever the distance, Max saw shapes up ahead. At first he couldn't tell what they were, but as he, the other cadets and Darius drew closer, he could make out a tall upright pole with a cable running along its top. A rickety-looking chair moved silently along it, up into the mountains. The chair lift was, of course, empty. Nobody would be heading up in this weather; Max was surprised it was still running. The chair-lift station came into view. It was a simple place. There was a covered area, like an extended bus shelter. Here, the descending chairs turned a hundred and eighty degrees through a mechanical pulley system before ascending again. There was a tiny hut, which looked like a control centre. The chair-lift area was chained off and several signs were fixed to the chain. They read, in various languages: 'Hazardous weather conditions: strictly no access to the slopes.'

The cadets stopped and looked at each other. 'Why is it still moving?' Abby said.

'So people can get down from the slopes,' Lukas replied.

'Should we get on?' Sami asked. As he spoke, there was another roll of thunder and a gust of wind.

'No,' Max said. 'It'll be too dangerous up there . . .'

But as he spoke, he saw something: a red dot dancing on Lukas's chest. Lukas was facing the direction they had been running, which meant another gunman was approaching from the opposite direction. And he had them in his sights. Max threw himself at Lukas and they hit the ground just as a bullet whizzed over them.

'We need to get on the lift!' Abby shouted. Max didn't argue. He and Darius scrambled up from the snow and together the group hurtled over the turnstile towards the chair lifts. There was room for two on each lift. They were moving excruciatingly slowly. Max hustled Darius onto the first lift with Lili, pulling down the safety bar with a clunk. Lukas and Sami went next, and finally Max and Abby. The chair swayed precariously as they were lifted into the air. Looking ahead, Max was relieved to see that Lili and Darius's chair had already vanished into the blizzard, which put them out sight of the gunmen. But to his right and left, Max could see grey figures approaching, two from one side, two from the other. He made a mental adjustment: at least four people were pursuing them. He and Abby were five metres high before they remembered to slam down their own safety bar. 'Duck!' he told Abby. 'Make a small target. They might –'

Fire.

Yet another bullet flew above them, just missing their heads. Max and Abby kept low. Only when the chair lift had taken them another ten metres did Max risk looking back down. The chair-lift station was out of sight. He could make out five empty chairs below them before he lost visibility.

'Are they following?' Abby whispered.

'I don't know,' said Max. 'I can't see.'

They rose higher. A terrible chill enveloped them. As they ascended, a biting wind started to howl. It felt like it was cutting into Max's skin, and it made their chair rock precariously. He gripped the safety bar and dared to look down. The ground was out of sight. It could have been ten metres or a hundred metres below them. He felt a wave of vertigo, and gripped the safety bar even harder. All he could see was swirling snow all around. He shivered: a cold shiver, and a fearful one.

'Well,' Abby said quietly, 'this is romantic.' There was no trace of the usual humour in her voice. It was as numb as Max's hands.

'I don't know how far up this lift takes us,' Max said.

'Does it matter?' Abby replied. 'They can shoot us just as easily at four thousand feet as at one thousand.'

'The higher we go, the colder it will be,' Max said. 'That makes a difference, if we have to hide.'

'You think they're following us, then?'

He looked back and down, along the line of the chair lift. As he did so, there was another crash of lightning and boom of thunder. It illuminated everything around them. Max saw, for an instant, figures on the lower chair lifts, perhaps thirty metres away.

'Yeah,' Max said, his voice grim. 'They're following us. And my bet is they won't stop following us until they've done what they want.'

The cable above them creaked ominously. 'Not going to lie,' Abby said. 'I'm not enjoying this.'

'Gather your strength,' Max said. 'It's going to be tough at the top.' He pulled out his phone again, checking for service so they could alert Hector, Woody and Angel to their situation. There was nothing.

Silence. Just the creak of the overhead cable and the moan of the wind. A juddering musical rattle each time they passed one of the metal pylons.

A minute passed.

Two minutes.

Three. The temperature was still dropping noticeably. The snow was icier, the visibility poorer. Max found he had to breathe more deeply, because the air was less rich in oxygen.

And then, emerging from the snow up ahead, he saw the chair-lift station approaching. The others were standing in a huddle, waiting for them. As Max and Abby's chair drew up alongside them, Lukas helped them raise the security bar.

'They following?' he asked as his friends jumped off.

Max nodded and looked around quickly. There was a small control hut just beyond the point where the chair lifts turned to descend through a mechanical pulley system identical to the one they had seen at ground level. He ran over to the hut and tried to open the front door. It was locked. No way in. There was a shovel leaning against the wall. It was obviously there so people could clear snow away if they needed to. Maybe he could use it to jemmy the door open. No. It would just break the shovel. Acid fear rose in his gut. The other chair lifts were relentlessly ascending, clattering as they hit the station. Max reckoned they had a less than a minute to get away before the assassins arrived . . .

'What are we supposed to do?' Darius shouted, his voice thin and reedy in the wind.

'We've got to stop the lift!' Lili shouted.

The other cadets were banging on the door of the control hut, trying to get in. Max ran around the hut and found, leaning against an external wall, three sets of skis and ski poles half covered in snow. He grabbed one of the poles and sprinted back to the chair-lift station. The chairs were still rising inexorably. Although he could not yet see the ones that carried their pursuers, he knew it was only a matter of seconds.

He raised the ski pole above his right shoulder and, using all the force he could muster, jammed it into one of the pulleys.

There was a metallic groaning sound as the chair lift ground to a halt. Max could feel his heart pumping. Now the mechanical sound of the lift had stopped, he was more aware of the wind and the snow. The others joined him, looking uncertainly at the ski pole.

'That won't hold them for long,' Lili said. 'The force of the lift will snap it soon enough. The chairs are going to start moving again.'

'So what do we do?' Sami said. 'Carry on trying to break into the hut, or get out of here?'

'We've got to get out of here,' Lukas said. 'We don't know how long it'll take to break into the hut, and we might not be able to stop the lift if we do. It might need a special key or something.'

Max nodded. He ran back to the hut, where he grabbed the shovel by the door, another two poles and a ski. Re-joining the others, he thrust a pole into a second pulley. 'That might

60

hold it a bit longer,' he said. He looked at the others. As if in confirmation, the chair lift groaned and the first pole shuddered.

'We need to stay close to each other,' Lili said. 'It'll be easy for us to get separated in these conditions.'

'Easy to be followed too,' said Lukas. 'They'll see our footprints in the snow.'

Max handed the shovel to Lukas. 'We might need that,' he said. He held up the ski. 'We'll walk in single file. I'll wipe our footprints with this as we go. It won't be perfect, but it might delay them for a bit.'

'Where are we going?' Darius said. He looked like he might cry.

'Somewhere where there aren't men trying to kill us,' Max replied. He handed his remaining ski pole to Abby. 'Look after this,' he said.

'What's it for?'

'Just in case.'

The pulleys groaned again.

'Let's get out of here,' he said.

They forged in single file away from the chair-lift station. Lukas went first, then Lili, Darius, Sami, Abby and finally Max, who walked backwards and scraped the ski over their footprints. The ski left an indentation, but Max reckoned the falling snow was heavy enough to cover it within two or three minutes. After thirty seconds, the chair lift had disappeared. After a minute, Max was completely disorientated. He kept looking back over his shoulder to check that Abby was still in view, but he had no idea in which direction they were travelling in the whiteout. All he knew was that they were moving steadily uphill.

He wondered if the ski poles were still holding. It was impossible to know. He decided that, now, speed was as important as stealth. As a group, they could travel much faster if Max was not wiping away their footprints. He discarded the ski and hurried through the snow to Abby.

'We're lost,' she said as they hurried along, following Sami. 'You know that, right?' She was still holding the spare ski pole.

'I know.'

'And it's going to get dark soon. We're talking plenty of degrees sub-zero.'

'I know.'

They walked on in silence for a few seconds.

'Ah well,' said Abby. 'I guess it'll give us the opportunity to snuggle up and get warm.'

And despite everything – despite the cold, and the danger, and the fear – Max blushed.

8

Snow Hole

There were two fire engines blocking the road where the tree had fallen, their lights flashing. The tree had almost burned itself out and the surrounding snow had stopped the flames from spreading. The wreck of the police car still smouldered. Seven firefighters went about their business, dousing the tree and car, and looking with horror at the two bodies in the front seats, burned to a crisp.

The firefighters were not the only people on the site. There were four other figures – three men and a woman – wearing snow gear, hot from running here through the snow, their expressions sick.

'I don't think it's them,' said Angel. 'In the car, I mean. They look like adults. Like they *were* adults, I guess.'

Hector turned to Alfie Grey. The former SAS man had bent down to retrieve something from the snow. He held it up. It was the spent casing of a handgun round. 'Nine millimetre,' he said. 'There's been gunfire here.'

'But no sign of bodies,' said Woody. He pointed along the road, past the smoking trees. 'That way.'

The firefighters shouted at them to stay clear. But the Watchers and Mr Grey ignored them. They powered past the fire engines and cleared the tree. Instantly they saw trails in the snow. Angel ran over to examine them. 'Six people came this way,' she called to the others. 'Then two people followed. You can see their tracks are very slightly fresher.'

They ran, following the footprints. After a kilometre, Woody found another 9mm casing in the snow. He exchanged anxious looks with his companions. Then they saw the chair-lift station. The chairs were stationary. Angel examined the footprints again. She pointed to the road on the other side of the station. 'Two more people came from that way,' she said. 'They approached the station. So did all the others.'

'So, if we're reading this right,' Hector said, 'the cadets and Darius were hemmed in. They had no other place to go, so they took the chair lift into the mountains.'

The others nodded their agreement.

Alfie Grey was looking up through the blizzard into the mountains. 'I know these peaks well,' he said quietly. 'This chair lift takes you up a good two thousand feet. Trust me, you don't want to be at altitude in these conditions. And with night falling –'

'We have to get up there,' said Angel.

'Alfie,' Hector said.

He turned.

'We need your help. Those kids are good, but they've got killers chasing them.'

'The chair lift's not working,' said Alfie. 'And we'll never get a chopper up there in these conditions. If we have to climb, it'll take most of the night. I can make sure we avoid avalanche-prone slopes and crevasses, but we'll need to get proper gear first.'

Hector barely took a moment to consider it. 'We climb,' he said. 'How long do you need to get the snow gear together?'

'There are shops in the town where I can buy what we need. Give me an hour.'

'Go,' Hector said. 'The sooner you return, the sooner we can get started.'

'I'll come and help,' Woody said. Alfie nodded and the two men ran back along the road into Zermatt.

'We've taught them well,' Angel said, as she and Hector looked through the blizzard up the slope. She sounded like she was persuading herself of something.

'They've got two enemies up there,' Hector said. 'The assassins and the mountains. In conditions like these, I don't know which is more deadly.'

They fell silent as they waited for the others to return.

The light was fading. The cadets had to stay closer to remain in sight of one another. The temperature was still dropping, and they were moving more slowly. Max's extremities were growing numb. The wind seemed to cut into him. He knew that they wouldn't be able to carry on like this for much longer. They needed shelter, but there was none. Just snow, everywhere.

Then Darius tripped and fell. The cadets congregated around him. He scrambled to his feet, but he was shivering badly.

'We need to get warm,' Lukas said. He had to speak loudly to be heard over the wind.

'We've got more chance of getting warm in a freezer,' Abby said. Her lips had a blue tinge to them.

'Maybe not,' Max said. He thought he had seen something through the blizzard. 'You still got that ski pole?'

Abby held it up.

'That way.' Max pointed.

They continued tramping through the snow. In less than a minute, the object Max had seen became clearer. It was a cliff face, perhaps thirty metres high. The pale rock was exposed. It was windward, so it afforded no cover. But snow was drifting up against its base. 'Lukas has a shovel,' he shouted to the others. 'We can dig a snow cave.'

'Are you crazy?' said Darius. His teeth were chattering.

'He's right,' Lili said. 'If we do it properly, it will insulate us and hide us at the same time. But we need to get started. I don't think we've got more than an hour of daylight left.'

None of the cadets had ever dug a snow hole before, but they knew the theory. They needed to dig a tunnel at an upwards angle into the drifted snow then, once inside, excavate a cavity big enough for them all. The theory was easy. In practice, it was a whole lot harder. They only had one spade, so they took it in turns to dig. Those who were not digging kept their hands tucked into their armpits for warmth.

It was strenuous work. When it was his turn with the spade, Max found himself sweating and he removed his jacket.

'Are you *crazy*?' Darius said for the second time.

'I might not know anything about calculus,' Max replied,

'but I know something about survival. I'm starting to sweat. That can be dangerous in the cold. Your clothes get wet and that brings your body temperature down. When it's sub-zero, wet means dead.'

That silenced Darius. He nodded mutely and left Max to get back to work.

It took more than an hour to excavate the snow hole. Max gave Darius the job of using the excavated snow to build a windbreak in front of the entrance. It was almost dark by the time the cadets had dug a cavity big enough for the six of them to climb into. Darius, shivering, looked uncertainly at the rough tunnel. He wasn't the only one who didn't seem entirely sure that this was the right call. Sami and Lukas had worked hard at excavating the snow hole, but now they were looking at the entrance, shaking their heads.

'We're going to freeze,' Lukas said, his forehead creased into a frown.

'Only if we stay out here. Our bodies generate heat. Out here, it just gets lost into the air. Inside, the snow acts as an insulator. It should keep us above zero.'

'Sounds cosy,' Abby said. She looked around for the spare ski pole she had left in the snow, and picked it up.

'No. We're in for a long night. But it's better than being out in the open.'

The cadets and Darius crawled through the tunnel and into the snow hole. The upward angle of the tunnel meant that cold air would sink down it. It was pitch black inside the hole, but they were able to use their phone torches to give themselves a little light, even if they couldn't make any calls. They cast an eerie light, and the sound of the cadets moving around in the hole was strangely muffled. The hole was awkwardly small. Even kneeling, they had to bend over to stop their heads brushing the ceiling. There was hardly any room to move around.

Max had seen to it that the floor of the hole was on two levels. 'We need to sit on the higher level,' he said. 'It'll be warmer there, because the cold air will sink into the lower part. It's called a cold trench. It'll keep us half a degree warmer if we sit above it. I know it doesn't sound much, but it'll make a big difference.' He looked around the curved interior wall of the hole. It was rough and uneven. 'We need to smooth off the inside,' he said. 'Otherwise we'll get water dripping on us. Use your coats so you don't have to touch the snow with your hands.' While the others got to work, removing their coats and using them to smooth the interior wall, Max scooped up enough snow to fashion a hard block that he fitted into the opening of the tunnel, blocking their way in and out.

'Wait,' said Darius. 'There's no way for air to get in and out. We'll suffocate.' In the light of the phones, he looked terribly scared.

'No, we won't,' Max said. He found the spare ski pole that Abby had brought into the hole. Gripping it by its pointed end, he drove the handle hard into the roof of the snow hole. It took a couple of goes before he could be sure it was poking out into the night air. He pulled it back in. 'There,' he said. 'Ventilation. We can breathe.'

Max, Abby and Sami removed their coats and spread them over the floor of the upper level. The six of them sat on the coats, which insulated them from the icy coldness of the snow.

They spread their remaining coats over their laps, like one enormous blanket.

'We should turn off our phones,' said Lili. 'To preserve the battery. We might get a signal in the morning.'

They killed the lights and were plunged into utter darkness. There wasn't even any moonlight through the ventilation hole. The teenagers fell into a deep silence. Max could just make out the sound of the wind howling outside. He felt a bite of anxiety as he pictured the rock face above them. The snow falling in the darkness, blocking all visibility. The horror of seeing the little red dot of a laser sight nearby.

He didn't know what they would do in the morning. Try to get off the mountain? Stay hidden? They couldn't make any decisions until the sun came up and they had a chance to evaluate the conditions. For now, they just had to focus on getting through the night.

Darius's voice pierced the silence. 'I wish you would tell me who you are.'

No one replied. The silence became heavier. The wind howled outside. Abby snuggled up to Max. He put his arm around her shoulders and focused on staying warm.

9

Reg

Time passes slowly when your friends are in danger.

Alfie Grey took no more than the hour he had promised to buy equipment but, to Hector and Angel, it felt like a day. They kept moving at the foot of the chair lift, trying to keep warm. Not easy. The light was failing. There was no let-up in the snowfall, and the wind was growing strong enough to blow powder from the ground. Snow collected in Hector's beard and Angel's red hair was turning a frosty white. There was the occasional flare of lightning overhead, and distant rumbles of thunder. Only a fool would risk climbing in these conditions. A fool, or a desperate person.

They checked their phones every few minutes, but it was no good. Zero service. It was a relief when they saw Alfie and Woody returning through the blizzard. They ran to meet them. The two men were laden with gear: rucksacks. Snow boots. Walking poles. Powerful head torches. Protective coats, hats and gloves. Snow goggles. Torches. Binoculars. High-energy snacks.

'We've got a big problem,' Alfie shouted. 'The forecast is for this storm to get worse overnight. Also, all the local cellular masts have been taken out by the lightning strikes. Nobody here is going to be able to use their phone for days. Finding those kids is going to be like finding a needle in a haystack.'

'Look on the bright side,' Hector said, with an expression that suggested he was doing anything but. 'It'll be more difficult for the assassins to locate them too.'

'They have a head start on us,' Woody reminded him.

They shared the equipment out, quickly and wordlessly, protecting themselves from the elements with layers of warm clothing. When they were ready, Alfie Grey turned to them. He had to shout to be heard over the wind.

'I don't want to teach my grandmother to suck eggs,' he told them, 'but I know these slopes well. I should take the lead. Anyone have a problem with that?'

Nobody did.

Alfie handed around sachets of high-energy gel. 'Eat these,' he shouted. 'Then we'll get moving.'

The gels tasted of orange. The team swallowed them in a few seconds, then they activated their head torches and moved back towards the chair-lift station. Hector pointed at the overhead cable that disappeared into the blizzard-filled darkness. 'Should we follow the same route as the lift?' he said. It would make sense, because it would guide them in the right direction.

Alfie shook his head. 'Not a good plan. The snow drifts pretty deep along that route, and there are several crevasses along the way.'

71

Crevasses: deep fissures beneath the snow, almost impossible to detect until you fell into one. In conditions like these, avoiding crevasses was a priority. In any case, the more Hector thought about it, the less keen he was on staying too close to the chair lift. They couldn't avoid using their head torches, which meant they could be seen from a distance. There was a high chance that the guys pursuing the cadets would be near the lift. It would be safer for Hector and the team to choose a different route.

They moved in single file: Alfie, Hector, Angel then Woody. The beams from their head torches struggled to penetrate the blizzard. They had little more than ten metres of visibility, and the snowfall meant that their surroundings were almost identical in all directions at all times. Without Alfie's expertise and local knowledge, they'd have been lost in minutes.

The slope was steep and they climbed slowly for many reasons. Before each step, they felt the way ahead with their walking poles. Often they were battling into the wind, which blew stinging snow in their faces. As the conditions deteriorated, they roped up. They understood the importance of sticking close. They moved slowly.

As the night wore on and their altitude increased, the air grew colder. They reached a craggy outcrop and stopped to check on each other and to rest for a moment. Their head torches were the only part of them not dusted in snow: the faint warmth of the bulb melted the flakes into beads of water as they settled. They stood in a circle, squinting in the light of each other's torches, the wind whipping about them.

'If it's this bad here,' Angel shouted over the howling, 'it'll be worse higher up where the cadets are. They're not equipped for these conditions. I'm scared they won't make it through the night.'

'If they're smart,' Hector shouted back, 'and they are, they'll have holed up.' He looked around, peering into the driving snow. 'Wish we could do the same. But we can't. Let's keep moving.'

They struggled on. The conditions worsened. Their rate of ascent slowed. From time to time, Alfie took a compass from his pack and checked their bearings. It was an almost impossible task without some point of reference, of which there seemed to be none. But Hector understood that Alfie knew these slopes intimately and could orientate himself by features that were invisible to the others: a snow-covered mound of rock, a sudden change in the gradient, a solitary tree. He was thankful Alfie was there. Under ordinary circumstances, coincidences made Hector nervous. On this occasion, he was grateful that, by chance, he had encountered his old army mate. Alfie was one of the best SAS men Hector had ever known, and he knew they were lucky to have his expertise.

As he climbed, he thought. Back in the day, Hector, Alfie and Max's dad Reg had been an inseparable trio. They'd come up through the ranks together, passed SAS selection together, served together, fought together. After Reg's death in Afghanistan, their paths had diverged. It was almost as if, now that Reg was no longer with them, it was too painful for Hector and Alfie to be together. It brought back too many memories. Neither Hector nor Alfie had said as much. But Hector knew Alfie well, and he recognised something in his old friend. Alfie was a determined man, but right now he seemed obsessed. Hector understood. Reg Johnson's son's life was in danger. Alfie was prepared to do anything to help him, even to the point of compromising his own safety.

That thought made him stop and look back to check on Woody and Angel. They were close, grim-faced and determined, forcing themselves further up the mountain. Alfie wasn't the only person putting himself at risk. They would all give whatever they had to rescue the cadets. Trouble was, it might not be enough.

The wind screamed murderously. It felt as if it was spinning all around them, and the blizzard's dance had a different quality: the snow fell more thickly and more randomly. Hector found it disorientating. He wasn't the only one. Alfie raised one hand to indicate that they should stop. They halted. Alfie turned.

'I can't navigate in these conditions!' he shouted. 'We'll have to wait for this wind to subside!'

'But the others!' Angel shouted.

'We do what Alfie says,' Hector told her. Woody and Angel looked mutinous, but Hector's urge to get to the cadets was just as strong as theirs. They knew he wouldn't risk a delay if it wasn't absolutely necessary.

There was a more immediate problem: they couldn't just wait here, exposed to the elements. Alfie had a solution. He struck off at a 300-degree bearing to their previous direction of travel. Ten minutes later, they came to a small hut. It wasn't much bigger than a garden shed, and snow had drifted against one side, almost to the roof, which was laden anyway. The door was accessible though. All they had to do was clear a couple of feet of snow from the base, then they shuffled inside.

There was nothing in the hut. No furniture, no heat source. Although it was still very cold, it protected them from the chill of the wind, which was a great relief.

'What is this?' Woody asked. They could still hear the wind, but it wasn't so deafening and they didn't have to raise their voices quite so much.

'It's a refuge hut,' Alfie said, turning off his head torch. 'They're dotted around these mountains. Some of them are big and well equipped. Not this one, but it serves a purpose. Only one of us needs to keep their torch on in here. Save power.'

Everyone except Hector turned off their head torch.

'How long do we have to wait?' Angel demanded.

'I understand how impatient you are,' Alfie said. 'I get it, really I do. But we can't help those kids if we get lost in the storm and die of exposure or come across an avalanche slope or fall into a crevasse.'

'You *don't* get it,' Angel said. 'Those "kids", as you call them . . .'

She fell silent. Alfie had gripped her arm.

'I *get* it,' he growled, and this time nobody took issue with him. 'I think we'll be here half an hour, perhaps a bit longer. Weather is highly changeable in these mountains. The storm's going nowhere for a few hours, but the wind might subside. This is the best place for us for now, trust me. I suggest you sit on the floor, keep warm and gather your strength. We've got a lot of climbing ahead of us.'

There was no more argument. The team huddled on the floor and listened to the wind whipping around the hut. Hector glanced at Alfie. 'He's his father's son,' he said. 'Max, I mean.

He doesn't just look like him. Sometimes I have to stop myself from thinking Reg is in the room with me.'

Alfie nodded. 'When I first saw him, at the school, I thought I was seeing a ghost.' There was a moment of silence. 'Does he know how his parents died?'

Hector nodded. 'I didn't want to tell him. I thought maybe it was better if he didn't know.' He stared ruefully into the middle distance. 'Or maybe I was just scared of the truth.'

'How did Reg die?' Angel said.

'He was captured in Afghanistan,' Hector said. 'I was his commanding officer at the time, and Alfie's too. Not that it made any difference between the three of us. Max's mum Maddie was in the UK looking after Max, who was a baby. She was an intelligence officer – one of the best. As soon as she heard Reg was missing, she flew straight out to Afghanistan. She thought she could help by using her contacts to locate him. She was right. Turned out Reg was being held in a cave system near the border with Pakistan. We ordered a rescue mission. Me, Alfie, Maddie and a team of the best guys we could put our hands on.' Hector looked at the floor and sighed.

'What happened?' Woody asked quietly.

Alfie took over telling the story. Hector was glad. He didn't have the stomach for it.

'Reg and Maddie were killed, along with a lot of other guys.' Alfie sniffed. 'Worst day of my life. I left the army soon after that. Couldn't continue, somehow. We all blamed ourselves for the failure of the mission. For Reg and Maddie's deaths.'

'It was my fault,' Hector said. His voice cracked. 'If I had taken more time to plan the raid . . .'

'You did what you had to do, Hector,' Alfie said. He sounded strict. 'The longer we left it, the smaller the chance we'd find Reg alive. And as for our strategy . . .' His voice trailed off.

'What?' Angel said.

'It was almost like they knew we were coming,' Hector said. 'Those of us who lived were damn lucky. It was a massacre.'

Silence fell on the hut. It lasted for several minutes, broken only by the howling of the wind outside. Then the quality of the howling changed. It was just as loud, but somehow it didn't seem to resonate in the same way.

'The wind has changed,' Alfie said, switching on his head torch. 'We can carry on.'

The team left the refuge hut and continued their treacherous climb.

10

Snowpack

It was the longest night of Max's life.

Proper sleep was impossible. The snow hole kept their temperatures above freezing by insulating the warmth of their bodies, but it was still spirit-sappingly cold. The cadets and Darius lay close to each other. If Max drifted off occasionally, it was never for more than a few minutes. The cold always brought him back to consciousness. He was aware, from the way his friends kept jolting in the darkness, that their experience was the same.

It was completely dark in the snow hole. Every hour or so, Max would use his phone torch to find the ski pole and poke it through the ventilation hole. The hole offered no light, only sound. As Max lay in the darkness, he could hear the wail of the wind, deadened by the thick walls of the snow hole. It was horribly clear to him that they would not be able to hear anybody approaching. Even though, from a survival perspective, it had been the right call to bury themselves in the snow, they were vulnerable from a tactical perspective. They had no exit routes. They were sitting ducks.

No wonder none of them could sleep.

There wasn't one particular moment when Max realised the wind had abated. It happened gradually. The moment he realised they were lying in complete silence, he panicked. Had the blizzard covered the ventilation hole? He poked the ski pole through it. No sound. The storm had calmed, at least for now. He checked the time. Five minutes to four. Dawn was arriving. He lay back down with the others, chilled to his core.

'I feel like I'm never going to be warm again,' said Abby, snuggling up to Max.

'Has anybody else been awake all night?' Sami asked.

There was a murmur of agreement from the other cadets, but not from Darius. Max became aware of a breathy, snuffling sound. Darius was crying. Nobody mentioned it. They all waited patiently until he stopped.

'We shouldn't wait until full light to get out of here,' Lili said. 'We'll be too visible if the assassins are nearby.'

'Agreed,' Max said. 'As soon as it starts to get light, we'll move.'

'Move where?' said Lukas. 'We need a plan. That storm could come back any minute. We can't just wander around the mountains in these temperatures without the proper gear. We'll be dead by nightfall.'

Lukas's brutal assessment silenced them for a minute.

'The assassins will be looking for us,' Abby said. 'We need to think like them. What would they expect us to do?'

'They'll think we're just a bunch of scared kids who got

lucky,' said Lili. 'They'll be thinking that we're cold and terrified and that we'll want to get back down to Zermatt and safety as quickly as possible.'

'They'd be right,' Abby muttered.

'I agree with Lili,' Max said. 'If I was them, I'd make sure that someone was watching every way off the slopes. We don't know how many of them there are. We only saw three people chasing us, but they could have loads more at their disposal.'

There was another silence as they digested Max's words.

'We need to keep climbing, don't we?' Sami said.

'It's the safest option,' Lili agreed.

'We don't have the proper equipment,' Lukas argued. 'We can take our chances with the assassins. We can't take our chances with the mountains. They're more powerful than any of us.'

He was right. They were all right. None of the options available to them was good.

'I have another idea,' Max said. 'I think we need to find a refuge hut.'

'What's that?' Sami said.

'I was reading up on the way out here. Apparently there are these huts dotted around the slopes. Some of them are really quite big – like hostels. If we can find one, we can shelter. There might even be emergency comms equipment for us to contact the Watchers or Mountain Rescue. If it comes to it, we can put in defensive measures. I mean, I don't know where these huts are, but we should try to find one, right?'

'Wouldn't the assassins expect us to do that?'

'I don't think so. They're going to think they're better than us, remember. That we're running scared. And even if they don't, I'd feel safer with a solid wall between us and their firearms.'

Nobody disagreed. They fell into another silence.

It was hard to judge the passing of time in the darkness. Max kept his phone switched off to preserve the battery, but he estimated that it was about half an hour later that the ventilation hole became faintly visible: a tiny circular patch that gradually allowed a narrow beam of grey light in through the ceiling of the snow hole.

The cadets sat up. Although Max could only see their silhouettes, he could identify each of them. He could identify Darius too. He was hunched over, and he looked as though he was hugging himself. It was plain that he was not coping as well as the others with the cold. Another reason to get him to a refuge hut.

Max crawled to the snow hole's entrance. The block of snow he had used to seal the entrance had frozen hard and stuck to the walls surrounding it. He had to loosen it with the tips of his numb fingers. They became so cold that they almost felt separate to his body, but eventually the block came away and they were able to crawl out.

The hush that surrounded them was even deeper than the snow. A profound, sinister quiet that unnerved Max as he stood outside the snow hole with the others, scanning the area. There was barely any daylight – just a gloomy greyness and no sign of the sun – but the snow seemed to glow all around them. The cliff face loomed in the grey light like a giant watching over them. It occurred to Max that, vast though it was, this cliff face was just a tiny speck on the mountain ranges that surrounded them. He felt tiny and insignificant. Looking away from the cliff face, the terrain sloped gently before falling away sharply. Max shuddered. Last night, they had been a stone's throw from a sheer drop. If the weather deteriorated again, they would have to be much more careful.

'Which way will we go?' Darius said. They were the first words he had spoken since the previous night. His teeth were chattering.

His back to the cliff, Max pointed left. 'We came from that direction,' he said. 'I suggest we follow the line of the cliff and see what we find. I'll lead. Lukas, I think you're the strongest of all of us. You should take the rear because you're least likely to fall behind. That way, we can be sure of sticking together. Don't forget the shovel. And remember, everyone: we can't help being exposed against the snow. If I see anyone, I'll raise one hand. That means drop to the ground and bury yourself in the snow.'

Darius stared at him and Max wondered if he'd understood. Lili walked up to her new friend and put an arm around his shoulders. 'We're going to be fine. Trust me. My friends and I have been in worse situations than this. We're going to make sure you're safe.' Her words seemed to have an effect. Darius stood a little straighter and he even managed to give Lili a smile.

Max led them away from the snow hole. The only sound was the crunch of their feet in the snow. It felt good to be moving. Max's body temperature increased. His extremities were still numb with cold, but at least he wasn't completely frozen. He could think more clearly and was convinced that locating a refuge hut was the right call. But he also now realised that it might not be as straightforward as he'd thought. The blizzard had erased all traces of their footprints from the previous night and the terrain was completely unfamiliar. After only a few minutes they had reached the end of the cliff. Snow undulated in all directions and mini-summits rose all around them. The sun was hidden behind thick cloud. Navigation was impossible. They were lost.

Max stopped, checked behind him. The others were close, separated from each other by less than five metres. He checked all around, his keen eyes searching for threats. But there was nothing. No movement. Nothing out of the ordinary. He couldn't allow himself to feel relieved. The cadets were out in the open. They were very visible against the white snow. They were easy targets.

Every few minutes he checked his phone, desperate to see the little bars that would indicate a signal. No luck. Comms were still down. They had no way of contacting the Watchers.

And so they continued through the snow. Although they were still looking for a refuge hut, Max stuck with their original plan and led them uphill wherever possible. They passed another rock face, not so high as the first but with an overhang that meant there was a narrow strip where the snow was only a few centimetres deep and even, in places, non-existent. They followed this strip as it led them higher into the mountains for a good fifteen minutes. Then the overhang disappeared and a narrow gully led them sharply upwards to the brow of a hill. Max stopped just short of it and waited for the others to catch up.

'Wait here,' he told them. 'I'll see what's in that direction.' He was so cold it was difficult to speak.

He lowered himself to the ground and crawled through the snow to the brow of the hill, keeping as low as possible to avoid being seen. As the vista revealed itself, he had to suppress a surge of excitement.

To his right, a broad slope headed down. He couldn't see the bottom of the slope because it faded into mist. At the far side, however, about a hundred metres away, was a building. It looked absurdly out of place up here in the mountains, with no road leading to it. It was two storeys high, with a steeply pitched roof. As Max watched it, a load of snow slipped from the roof and crashed silently to the ground. He crawled back down to the others, stood up and brushed the snow from his front, then told them what he'd seen. 'We just need to cross that slope first,' he said.

'Wait,' Lili said. 'How steep is it?'

'I'd say about forty degrees,' Max told her.

'Any trees?'

'No.'

'And it's just had a fresh layer of snow. We need to check it's not avalanche-prone.'

'How do we do that?' Darius asked.

'We need to do a snowpack test,' Lili said. 'We cut out a block of the snow and look at the layers. If we find a layer of loose powder, it means there's a high chance of an avalanche.' She looked around. 'Lukas, give me the shovel.'

He handed it over.

'Max, you come with me. The rest of you keep lookout. Whistle if you see anything suspicious. Otherwise be as quiet as possible. It's not just the assassins we need to worry about. If

84

that slope is avalanche-prone, a fall can be triggered by sound. We'll be as quick as we can.'

The others nodded, except Darius, who looked distressed at the idea of Lili leaving him, even for a short while. Abby noticed this and smiled at him. 'You stick with me,' she said, as Max and Lili lay down in the snow and crawled back to the brow of the hill. They took a moment to view the wide slope and the refuge hut on the far side, and to check for signs of danger. There were none, so they moved over the brow to the edge of the slope.

'We need to cut out a block about a metre cubed,' Lili said. She spoke very quietly.

'Right,' Max said. 'What then? I don't really know what we're looking for.'

'The snow builds up in layers over the year,' Lili explained. 'You get a heavy snowfall and the layer freezes. Then you get another snowfall and another. It makes all these different layers, but they have different consistencies. Some of them are like sheets of ice. Some of them are all powdery, like sugar. If you get a lot of sugar down the bottom of the snowpack, or if you get a very icy layer above a very sugary layer, it means there's a high risk of avalanche.'

The spade made a swishing, slicing sound as Max cut through the snow. It took a good twenty minutes to excavate a block but, once they had, Max could tell at a glance that it wasn't good.

'Here,' Lili said. She was pointing to a layer at the bottom of the snowpack: a good ten centimetres of powdery snow that crumbled away at the slightest touch. Above that was

85

a sturdy layer of ice, five centimetres thick. And above that, more powder. Max looked back across the broad slope and tried to imagine the layers of snow sliding into a full-blown avalanche. The thought made him shudder. The weight of all that snow. The forces involved. Again he felt insignificant against the awesome power of the natural world.

Then he looked over at the refuge hut. It might be separated from them by a wide slope that could avalanche at any moment, but it was their only chance of shelter and safety.

'We have to cross the slope, don't we?' said Lili.

Max nodded. 'Yeah,' he said. 'We have to cross the slope.'

11

The Slope

'We need to do this one by one,' Lili said.

She and Max had returned to the other cadets. They had explained the result of their snowpack test and were met with some worried expressions. Everyone agreed, however, that they needed to reach the refuge hut.

'Why?' Darius said. 'I'd feel better if we stuck together.'

'We all would,' Lili agreed. 'But that's not the smart move. The slightest movement can trigger an avalanche. The tiniest noise or vibration. If we cross the slope in a group, our footfall will cause more intense vibrations. Even if we go individually, we have to tread very lightly. But we each need to cross as quickly as possible. The longer we're on the slope, the higher the risk.'

Silence.

'We should cross at the top of the slope,' Lili continued. 'An avalanche can start at any point, so it's better to have less snow above you.'

'What if there *is* an avalanche?' Darius asked.

'If the snow starts to move, you need to make sure you're above it. If you get caught up in the avalanche, your best bet is to get on your back and keep your head above the snow by doing a swimming backstroke movement with your arms.'

'And if you can't keep your head above the snow?'

Lili had no answer to that.

'Let's move then,' Max said. 'Sooner we get this done, the better.'

It took half an hour to reach the top of the slope. They located a ridge that took them that way, where the sides fell sharply away and the snow was a little shallower along the ridge line. At the top of the slope, they paused and eyed it uncertainly.

'I'll go first,' Max said. Before anybody could stop him, he stepped onto the slope.

He sank ankle-deep into the snow. His boots made an ominous crunching sound. He couldn't help thinking about the sugary layers of powder in the snowpack, and he glanced nervously down and across the slope, once more imagining the awesome power of an avalanche. The thought paralysed him for a moment, but then Lili hissed at him.

'Move faster!'

He took another step, then another, moving as quickly and lightly as possible. He forced himself to watch the terrain in front of him, and the refuge hut, rather than look down the slope. Even then, it felt as though it took hours to cross, although it was only a few minutes. By the time he reached the far side, where the terrain levelled out as it approached the refuge hut, he was sweating heavily despite the cold. He turned and looked back the way he'd come, then he raised one hand to the others, to indicate that he was safe.

Lukas went next. It seemed to Max that he crossed much more quickly. He was the biggest of the cadets, and Max found himself watching the powder anxiously as he strode across the top of the slope. Lukas might have been big, but he was deft. He followed Max's footprints and there was no sign of any snow sliding down the slope. Lukas was frowning and silent when he arrived at the other side. Max knew him well and could tell his friend was stressed.

'I don't know if Darius is going to make it,' Lukas said.

Max could see what he meant. On the other side of the slope, Lili seemed to be talking intently to the Iranian boy. He could tell by her body language that she was trying to encourage him. Max suppressed a twinge of impatience. The cadets were used to perilous situations. They had trained hard so they could trust their skill and instincts under pressure. Darius had none of those advantages. No wonder he was more fearful than the rest of them.

It was agonising to watch. Darius had none of Lukas's deftness. His arms were stretched out as though he was walking a tightrope. He paused after each step and stared down the slope. On several occasions, he seemed completely unstable and Max thought he might fall. He realised he was holding his breath, waiting for disaster . . .

It didn't come. Darius's crossing was slow, clumsy and excruciating for them all, but he made it, and even managed a smile when Max offered him some encouraging words.

Abby came next. Her face was a model of concentration. She moved swiftly, but with a no-nonsense gait. When she reached Max and the others, she started singing 'Do You Want to Build a Snowman?' Darius looked confused and Max had to smile.

Sami next. He was so slight that he seemed to dance across the slope. He joined them in almost no time at all.

Which left Lili, the last of them. She moved with characteristic care, following the footprints of the others. Max trusted her to make it across safely. He turned to check out the refuge hut . . .

Abby screamed. The scream was short and sharp, and she stifled it almost immediately. Max spun back around and his stomach turned to lead. Lili was halfway across. She was facing downhill, and a huge chunk of snow was sliding from in front of her. It seemed to move in slow motion, gathering more snow as it crawled down the slope in sinister silence.

And then it stopped.

Nobody moved. Max was holding his breath. Lili was like a statue, arms out as though ready to do the backstroke. She stayed like that for a full thirty seconds. Then, slowly, gingerly, she turned to face them. Max's instinct was to race back across the slope to help her. He sensed that the others felt the same. But that would be the worst thing to do. The situation required less movement, not more. Lili would understand that.

Max's heart thumped in his chest as he watched her approach. Her movements were calm but, every time she put a foot to the snow, Max winced as though the mountains themselves were trembling. He could hear Abby's shaky breathing. Sami muttered something to himself that Max couldn't make out. A prayer, maybe? He wondered if he should pray too.

The only person who didn't seem nervous was Lili. Sure, she moved slowly and with an abundance of care. Sure, there was a small frown of concentration on her face. But Max had the impression she was using her mind as much as her body as she made tiny, cat-like movements and approached without triggering any more falls of snow.

Max exhaled loudly when she reached them. He wasn't the only one. Abby silently hugged her friend, then they both looked embarrassed. Max reminded himself that they hadn't reached safety yet. The refuge hut was still about thirty metres away. He swept the area for threats one more time, then led the others towards the hut.

In fact, 'hut' was the wrong word. It looked more like a house, with its steeply pitched roof and twee detailing around the windows. Snow had drifted almost up to the lowest window at the front, but there was an accessible door at the side. Max headed towards it, noting that there were no footprints in the snow. They were the first to approach the house that morning. That didn't mean, of course, that it was deserted. They would have to be careful as they entered.

The door was unlocked. It opened inward with a creak that seemed to echo around the mountains – or maybe it was just Max's nerves making it seem that way. They entered a large room that took up most of the ground floor. There were no lights and no heating. It was as cold inside as out. Threadbare sofas were dotted around the room, and coffee cups lay, abandoned, on the floor. A kitchen area to the left had a kettle and a hob. It had the air of a hostel, where people would hang out for the day if the weather was no good for skiing.

But today nobody was hanging out. This room, at least, was deserted.

There was a long wooden ladder on the floor.

'What's that for?' Lukas said, but nobody knew. Against the far wall was an open staircase. Max and Lukas headed towards it while the others moved to the front windows to survey the exterior. The stairs creaked even more than the door. Each footstep made Max wince. He couldn't keep his steps silent, no matter how hard he tried.

There was no landing. The stairs led to an open-plan first floor. It was full of stuff. There were some single beds and various large cupboards. Stashes of snow gear were piled here and there, and boxes were scattered around. None of these drew Max's attention. Because in the centre of the room, lying on his back, his arms and legs splayed, was a dead man.

Max knew he was dead, even from a distance. There was something about his leaden stillness – a thick, cold stillness that put ice in his veins. He didn't want to approach the dead man. At the same time, he couldn't stop himself. He and Lukas walked, side by side, to where he lay. They stood on either side of him and looked down.

He had been shot. The entry wound was in his forehead. Not bang in the centre, like in the movies, but a few centimetres to the right. The wound was ugly, a gory mess of ripped skin, dried frozen blood, shards of skull and a thick grey substance that Max guessed was brain matter. The rest of his face had a pale waxy pallor, except for his lips, which were tinged blue. There was frost in his hair and on his beard.

Max and Lukas stared at him. Their breath was visible in the cold air. Part of Max wanted to run – to get away from this gruesome sight and its implications as quickly as he could. Another part of him was analysing the scene. He couldn't see any scorch marks around the wound, and it was smaller than it would have been if the shot had been taken at very close range. He guessed that a 9mm round had inflicted the damage, and he pictured the gunman standing at the top of the staircase and taking the shot from about eight metres away. To aim successfully with a 9mm handgun at that range meant the shot had been a fluke – or the shooter was a professional. Max's money was on the latter.

Lukas bent down and touched the dead man's cheek. 'Ice cold,' he said. 'And look – some of the blood is frozen. He's been dead for a while.'

'There were no footprints approaching the hut,' Max said. 'I think this must have happened last night.'

They stared at each other. Were the assassins still here?

They turned and looked around the room. At the beds and the cupboards. At the boxes and the piles of gear. And at the door against the far wall, which Max hadn't noticed until now. He heard the others moving around downstairs, unaware of what they had found, and a hot prickle of fear melted the ice in his veins.

He turned back to Lukas and silently mouthed the words: 'We have to search the hut.'

12

Brave

They had no weapons. At least, not in the traditional sense. But the Watchers had taught the cadets that almost anything could be used as a weapon. Some ski poles leaned against a pile of equipment. Max and Lukas moved silently over and each grabbed a pole. Max felt it for balance. The best place to hold it, he decided, was three-quarters of the way up. It would give him the right combination of heft and swing, should he need it.

He could hear Abby's voice down below, though he couldn't make out what she was saying. He wanted to shout at her to keep quiet. Not the right call. If he made a noise, he would identify his and Lukas's position to anybody hiding up here. Instead, he tuned out the sound of their friends and focused on the closed door. He and Lukas approached it, stepping silently around the gear and boxes, gripping their ski poles. When they reached it, Lukas put one hand on the handle and prepared to yank it open. Max stood by the door frame and held his ski pole over his right shoulder, ready to swing it. His palms were sweating despite the cold. The pole felt less substantial than he'd hoped. Hardly a match for a killer with a gun. If there was anyone behind that door, he would have to strike hard and fast . . .

Lukas mouthed a countdown.

Three.

Two.

One.

He yanked the door open.

Silence.

There was a changing room beyond the door. Shower and toilet cubicles. Sinks. White ceramic tiles on the floor and walls that made it even icier than the rest of the hut. Max and Lukas entered gingerly. They checked each cubicle. Nobody was there. Max was feeling the cold again. He shivered. 'Back downstairs,' he mouthed, and Lukas nodded.

They avoided looking at the corpse as they passed it again. It occurred to Max that it didn't smell. The cold must be preserving the body. They hurried down the stairs to the ground floor. Abby was still talking. When she saw that they were carrying ski poles as weapons, she said: 'What the –'

Lukas hushed her with one finger to his lips. A chilly silence descended on the whole hut. Max pointed to each of the windows. Darius looked confused, but the cadets understood what he meant: check them. They followed his instruction, peering carefully out to look for any threats. Only when they had checked all the windows did Max speak.

'We've got a problem,' he said.

'You don't say,' Abby muttered.

'We've got a *bigger* problem. There's a corpse upstairs. He looks like a regular snowboarding dude, but –' He put two fingers to his forehead to describe what they'd seen. 'Not pretty,' he added. 'The guys chasing us are willing to kill anyone who gets in their way.'

'It doesn't look like the assassins are still here,' Lukas said. 'We think he was shot yesterday, and we've searched both rooms upstairs.'

'But it means they know about this refuge hut,' Lili said. 'They might have walked straight past us when we were in the snow hole. And that means they might come back here, if they need to.'

Lili's words settled on them like snowfall.

'I don't think there's any radio or comms equipment here,' Lukas said.

'So do we stay,' Sami said, 'and risk them coming back? Or do we clear out and risk the mountains?'

'I don't like either of those options,' Abby said.

'Me neither,' said Max. He moved over to the front window and looked out. He couldn't see the bottom of the avalanche-prone slope. It was lost in cloud. He checked through the kitchen window at the back of the hut. Here the snowy terrain was flatter, but visibility was still poor – thirty metres, maximum. It felt like the hut was surrounded by a shroud of mist which could be hiding anything. Or anyone.

'We should hedge our bets,' he said. 'We should stay here until our phones are working again and we can call for help. But in the meantime, there's a load of gear upstairs. We can get properly kitted out in case we need to leave in a hurry.

We need to keep up surveillance from all sides of the house. You guys do that. Lukas and I will go back upstairs and get the stuff.' He could tell from his friends' expressions that they were grateful not to have to join the corpse upstairs.

Max and Lukas headed back to the staircase. They were halfway up when Darius said, 'Wait!' He was walking towards them. 'I want to see,' he said.

Max narrowed his eyes. Then he nodded. 'Okay, if it's important to you.'

'It is.'

Darius followed them up the stairs and into the room on the first floor. He dug his nails anxiously into the palms of his hands and lingered at the top of the stairs, eyeing the body. Then he seemed to muster some courage. He walked quickly up to it and stared down at the entry wound.

'That's what they want to do to me?' he asked.

Max didn't reply. His silence said everything.

Darius frowned. 'Who are you?' he said. 'Why are you helping me?'

'It doesn't matter who we are,' Max said. 'But we're not going to let them get you, okay?'

Darius nodded. 'Thank you,' he said. 'I know I'm not as strong or as smart as you –'

'Hey.' Max grinned. 'Calculus!'

'Calculus won't help us here,' Darius said. 'There's different kinds of smart. Some are more useful than others. I'll try to be brave, but I'm so scared.'

'Good,' Max said. 'That means your brain is working properly. We're all scared. We'd be crazy if we weren't. But that's okay.

It keeps you sharp – and remember, it's impossible to be brave without being scared first.'

Darius nodded again. 'I think I'll go back downstairs now.'

'Do what the others say. Keep watching.'

Darius gave the corpse another glance, then left. Max took a deep breath. Familiarity made it no easier to be in the presence of the dead body. He tried not to look at it, but his eyes were magnetically drawn to the gruesome wound. He wondered who the man was. Just an innocent skier, he supposed, who had decided to sit out the storm in the refuge hut while his friends took the safer option and went back down the mountain. He'd just been in the wrong place at the wrong time. Max felt a seed of anger in his gut. It displaced some of the fear. These assassins were taking innocent lives, and nobody was doing anything to stop them.

At least, not yet.

'You do the boxes,' Max said to Lukas. 'I'll check the cupboards.'

They spent ten minutes rummaging through the gear in the room. It was disorganised and ramshackle, but there was an impressive array of equipment. They found warm outdoor clothing for them all, and six sturdy rucksacks. They found ski poles, binoculars, ropes, harnesses and carabiners. They found sachets of food and collapsible entrenching tools. They even found, at the back of one of the cupboards in a sealed plastic box, packs of avalanche explosives. There were three sets. Each was cylindrical and about thirty centimetres long, attached to a long yellow cable with a detonating device at one end. Max considered them for a moment before deciding that

98

they were too dangerous to carry in their packs. He put them safely back in the box.

Lukas looked especially pleased with a sturdy Leatherman multitool, which provided sharp knives, saws and screwdrivers in one. 'Always wanted one of these,' he said. He added it to the pile they had collected in the centre of the room, then they carried all the gear down to the ground floor.

'Is that food?' Abby said, eyeing the sealed foil packets in Max's arms. 'Jeez, I could eat a horse. I could eat several horses, come to think of it. I could eat a whole herd of horses. Do horses come in herds, or is that just sheep? I could eat a couple of sheep too, if they were going.'

Max threw her one of the packets. The others gathered around while he distributed them. When he opened his own packet, he realised how hungry he was. He gobbled down the cold food, squeezing it directly from the pack into his mouth – it was some kind of stew with potatoes – and immediately felt his body making use of the fuel.

'Get back to your lookout points,' he told the others. 'We need to keep watch at all times.'

The others returned to the windows, clearly torn between their hunger and the need to keep up surveillance. Max and Lukas divided up the gear. They all pulled on heavy snow trousers, thick fleeces and padded coats. Their existing hats and gloves were wet, and not as warm as those that Lukas had found in one of the boxes, so they changed them. Max filled the rucksacks with ropes, harnesses, food and other items so that they were approximately equal in weight, apart from the one intended for Darius, which was lighter. He hung the binoculars around his own neck and, when everything had been sorted, he joined Abby at one of the front windows.

'Is there any more of that food?' she asked.

'We should ration it,' Max said. 'We don't know what's ahead.'

'Ah, you're so sensible,' she said. She hesitated. 'That body up there,' she said. 'Was it . . . Max? What's wrong?'

Max had raised his binoculars to the window and was looking out. They were powerful, and the mist at the bottom of the avalanche-prone slope looked so close that felt he could reach out and touch it. He gave a low hiss. There was movement. It was barely noticeable. Just a slight discoloration in the mist, vaguely human in form. But there was no doubt in Max's mind that someone was out there. More than one person? He didn't know. Mountain Rescue? He wouldn't bet on it.

'Lock the door,' he said.

He was aware of one of the cadets running across the room to do it while he kept looking through the binoculars. The shapeless form had disappeared. Maybe Max had imagined it. He scanned left and right. Nothing. He was about to tell the cadets to stand down when he saw the shadow again. It was a little clearer this time. Definitely a person. 'We've got company,' he said.

He lowered the binoculars and peered through the window without the aid of the optics. He couldn't see anything. 'I think they're at least a hundred and fifty metres away,' he said.

'Are they getting closer?' Sami asked.

Max raised the binoculars again. The figure was there, more distinct. 'I think so,' he said.

'You reckon they know we're here?' said Lukas.

'If they don't, they will soon. We left footprints in the snow, remember?'

'Are we sure it's bad guys?' said Abby.

'Put it this way,' said Max, 'we're not sure it isn't.'

'If it's the assassins, we can't defend this place for long if they have weapons. And we know they do, right?'

'Right.'

Max knew that the weather was unpredictable in the mountains. As he lowered his binoculars, there was a break in the clouds and a sudden streak of sunlight cut through. The mist at the bottom of the avalanche-prone slope cleared almost magically. Max could see four figures, dressed in black. They were spread out. The ground between them was terraced with small rocky outcrops that would be easy to climb. Beyond the figures was a broad sweep of mountain scenery: snow and peaks and, lower down, trees. There was no view of Zermatt.

One of the figures raised something to his face. A scope. It was pointing directly at Max. The figure lowered the scope then pointed at the refuge hut.

Max turned to the others. 'They're coming,' he said.

13

Avalanche

The weather, and the visibility, improved by the second. The figures were hiking uphill. Max checked them through his binoculars. He could see weapons strapped to their bodies. They clearly meant business.

'Decision time,' Lukas said. 'Do we stay and defend ourselves? Or do we make a run for it while we still can?'

'Defend,' Abby and Lili said in unison.

'Run,' Sami and Darius said at the same time.

Max watched through the window, trying desperately to think. Four armed guys. Ruthless. Professional. Close. The truth was, the cadets' chances of survival were slim either way. The gunmen would soon gain entry to the refuge hut. And they had a good chance of catching up with the cadets if they ran. They were moving with relentless speed. One of them was even taking the risk of climbing along the edge of the avalanche-prone slope.

Max blinked. An idea occurred to him.

'Uh-oh,' said Abby. 'He's got that look on his face.'

'If they reach us,' Max said, 'they'll kill us and take Darius. There's no doubt about that, right?'

Grim-faced, the cadets nodded.

'So whatever we have to do to defend ourselves is okay.'

Complete agreement.

'And if it means the gunmen come to harm, they brought it on themselves.'

'What are you planning, Max?' Lili said.

He didn't answer. Instead, he ran up the stairs again. This time he managed to avoid staring at the corpse. He hurried to the cupboard where he'd found the avalanche explosives. He pulled out the plastic box and then took it back downstairs.

'Whatever you're planning,' Abby said, looking out of the window, 'you need to do it quickly. They'll be here in ten minutes. Less, maybe.'

Max took one of the charges out of the box.

'Is that what I think it is?' Lili said.

'I guess that depends what you think it is.'

'Avalanche explosive?'

He nodded.

'What is an avalanche explosive?' Darius said.

'They're used to set off avalanches to make the pistes safe. You put them at the top of the slope and detonate them. The sound waves from the explosion are supposed to trigger the avalanche.' She stared at Max. 'They're never used without checking there's nobody in the danger zone.'

'Never say never,' Max said. 'Does anybody disagree with what I'm about to do?'

'They're getting closer,' Abby said.

103

Max held the explosive in one hand and the detonator in the other. Lukas unlocked the door for him. Max ran outside. The glare of sun on snow stabbed at his eyeballs. From this position he couldn't see the figures approaching, but that didn't mean they couldn't see him. He had to move quickly. He forced his way through the thick snow and stopped as close as he dared to the avalanche-prone slope. He hurled the cylindrical explosive as far as he could. It spun in the air and landed silently twenty metres away. There was still plenty of slack in the cable leading to the detonator. He moved back, allowing the cable to snake along the ground in front of him. Once he had released all the slack, he didn't hesitate. He flicked the switch on the detonator.

The bang was not as loud as he'd expected. Max braced himself for the snow to start sliding.

It didn't.

Panic surged through him. If his plan didn't work, they'd left it too late to escape. They were dead.

He ran back to the refuge hut. Lukas was at the door, holding another explosive. He handed it to Max as Abby shouted, from inside, 'They're close!'

Max ran back to the slope and threw the explosive into the snow. Lukas joined him. He had the third and final explosive.

'Together?' he said. Max nodded.

Lukas hurled his explosive. It went a little further than Max's. They moved backwards together, letting out the slack as they went.

'On three,' Max said. 'One, two, three . . .'

They detonated: two cracks in quick succession. Max stared at the slope, willing the snow to move.

It didn't.

Not for five seconds.

And then it did.

Slowly at first. Barely perceptible. Like a raindrop gently trickling down a pane of glass. Then it gathered speed – and size. Max and Lukas hurried back to the refuge hut. By the time they reached it, the avalanche was in full flow. It had turned into a huge, billowing torrent. It reminded Max of waves crashing onto a beach, except it was strangely silent – and all the more terrifying for that.

He ran to the window. Looked out, straining to see the figures. There was no sign of them. Clouds of snow obscured his vision. He held his breath, waiting for the avalanche to subside. He was aware of the others congregating behind him, watching quietly.

It took a minute for everything to become still again and for the air to clear. Nobody said anything. Max raised his binoculars and scanned the bottom of the slope. There was no sign of the assassins.

'Are they –' Sami started to say.

Max was about to say, 'I think so,' when he saw movement. A single figure. It was little more than a grey dot at first, much further down the mountainside than before. The dot enlarged as the figure emerged from the snow. Max had to refocus the binoculars to see him sharply. His black clothes were snow-covered and he was brushing himself down.

A second figure appeared to his left and, immediately after that, a third. Their body language suggested that they were calling to each other and looking around for the fourth guy.

But the fourth guy was nowhere to be seen.

'One of them,' Max said quietly. He didn't feel good about what had just happened, even though the men were trying to kill them. 'I think the avalanche took one of them out. There are still three guys there, but they've been knocked further down the mountain.'

'Surely they're going to try and find their friend. If he's under the snow, they'll want to dig him out, won't they?'

'I'm not sure they think the way we do, Sami,' Max said. The men looked like they were regrouping. One of them pointed back up the mountainside towards the refuge hut. 'We've bought ourselves some time,' he said. 'But we need to get out of here. Quickly.'

'Which way?' Abby said.

'Nothing's changed,' Lili said. 'There's still a high chance that they'll have men waiting for us at all the major exits to the slopes. If we want to avoid them, we don't have a choice.'

'We have to climb,' Lukas said. 'And we can't rely on this weather holding. We've seen how quickly it changes.'

'Whatever we decide,' Max said, 'we need to decide it quickly.'

The men at the bottom of the slope were already advancing.

'*I've* made a decision,' said Darius. The cadets all looked at him. He was jutting out his chin a little, as if defying them to contradict him. 'You have risked your lives for me already. It is too much for me to expect. I'll go to these men. They can take me. Life in Iran is not so bad. I have friends there. And it would put you out of danger.'

'Darius,' said Abby, 'you're a sweet guy, but for a brainiac you can be awful dim.'

'What do you mean?'

'That plan has so many holes in it, we could use it as a sieve.' She held up her fingers to count them. 'One, life in Iran is going to be a whole lot different now you're the son of a wanted dissident. If you see anything but the inside of a cell, I'd be surprised. Two, your dad fled Iran because they wanted him to work on their nuclear programme. This is about more than us lot having a jaunt through the snow. And three – I'm going to level with you here, Darius, three's the one that tips it for me – you think those assassins are just going to leave us to build a snowman if we hand you over? Either we get away from them right now, or we're dead. I don't know about you, but I'm pretty certain which option I prefer.'

Darius frowned, clearly unsure how to respond.

'Abby's right,' Max said. 'So is Lili. We don't have a choice. We have to keep climbing and we have to do it now. Grab your packs. We're leaving.'

There were no more arguments. The cadets and Darius grabbed the rucksacks that Max and Lukas had packed for them. Seconds later they were filing out of the door.

It had been a long, difficult night. There had been moments when even Hector – rugged, determined Hector – doubted that they had made the right call. They had trudged silently up the mountainside, through the blizzard, for hour after hour. Even though he ordinarily prided himself on his ability to keep track of time, in conditions like these it became almost impossible. Their surroundings barely changed: the blizzard encircled them, as if they were living inside a snow globe.

The first rule of survival is to focus on your own safety – and sanity. If you don't, you've no chance of helping others. Hector kept reminding himself of this rule, but somehow could not obey it. His thoughts were with the cadets. He was harsh with them. Uncompromising. Unfriendly, sometimes. It was for a reason. He cared deeply for them. They were a remarkable group. Every time they were in danger – and danger was an occupational hazard for them – he felt as if his own life was at risk. That ache of dread burned in his stomach all night, and it burned hardest for Max. Hector knew that he would live with his guilt over Reg's death for the rest of his life. The responsibility for Max's safety was a burden he found difficult to bear. Max was his father's son, brave and smart. But brave, smart people die too. If it happened on Hector's watch, he would never forgive himself.

So he was thankful that Alfie Grey was with them. It wasn't just that he knew these slopes so well, although Hector was glad of that with every step they took. Alfie *understood*. He had known Reg almost as well as Hector had. He had lived through the trauma of losing him. They had not said as much to each other, but Hector knew that the same thoughts would be running through Alfie's mind. He was certain his old friend wanted to get to Max and the other cadets as quickly as possible.

And so, somehow, they mastered the elements. As dawn approached, the blizzard had lifted. Alfie raised a hand to stop them, then looked around and sniffed the air. 'It's a break in the weather,' he said, 'but it won't last. I'd say we have a couple of hours without snowfall. No more than that.'

'How can you tell?' Angel asked.

'Experience, I guess. You get a feel for it.'

The blizzard might have subsided, but visibility was still

poor. The slopes were shrouded in mist. As dawn arrived, the mist lent their surroundings a strange, spectral quality. An impenetrable greyness clung to them, and even Alfie began to doubt their progress. He stopped and peered through the opaque atmosphere, shaking his head and muttering to himself. Hector, Angel and Woody exchanged worried glances. The longer they delayed, the more danger the cadets were in. Hector didn't like to imagine how, or even if, they had survived the night, but every cell in his tired body wanted to keep moving. Stopping like this made him want to howl.

And then they heard the explosions.

There were three: a bang, then a thirty-second silence, then two more bangs in quick succession. It was impossible to tell how near or far away they were, because the sound echoed around the mountains. Alfie swore under his breath. 'What the hell was that?' he demanded of nobody in particular.

'It sounded like gunfire,' Woody said.

'Whatever it was, noises like that can trigger an avalanche,' Alfie said, and he squinted into the mist, as if by doing so he might be able to see further.

'We have to press on,' Hector said.

Alfie nodded and consulted a compass. He pointed uphill to their two o'clock. 'That way,' he said.

They had no option but to trust his sense of direction. They moved off at a faster pace through the mist.

Suddenly they emerged from the mist: above them, there was a patch of blue sky and the snow was blindingly white.

'See there!' Angel hissed, pointing further up the slope.

Hector followed with his eyes. A broad mountain vista

109

appeared before them. Slopes of different gradients. Outcrops and mountain peaks. There was a refuge hut, bigger than the one the Watchers had used for shelter. To the left was a steep slope where an avalanche had fallen. Beyond it was a gully that wound higher into the peaks.

And there were people.

To the naked eye, they were little more than dots. There were three individuals to one side of the avalanche slope. They were advancing towards the refuge hut. Beyond the hut were six tiny specks in single file, making their way up the gully. Hector scrambled in his pack to find his binoculars. He raised them to his eyes and focused quickly on the six dots. They were still too distant for him to be certain but, as he watched, the lead person looked back over his shoulder. He was black.

Lukas.

Hector had no opportunity to examine the others. The mist suddenly enveloped them again, solid and impenetrable. He turned to the others. 'It's them,' he said. 'Looks like they're being chased by three guys.'

'Three lucky guys,' Alfie said. 'That avalanche could have wiped them out. There could be more. We need to move carefully.'

'We need to move *quickly*,' Hector said.

'We can do that too,' Alfie agreed. 'And if we catch those men before they reach the youngsters . . .' He didn't finish his sentence, but his expression made his feelings clear.

Alfie Grey led the Watchers further up the mountain. They moved faster now: hunters following the scent of their prey.

14

Loop

The break in the weather was short-lived. The cadets were glad of the snow gear they'd scavenged from the refuge hut. They weren't glad of much else.

The assassins were chasing them. That much they knew. How fast they were moving, whether they were splitting up or sticking together, whether they knew the terrain and might be able to cut the cadets off; none of this was clear to them. The mist had returned. The blizzard was resuming. It was bad enough that they had to struggle with the elements. The thought that those men could be right behind them, or right in front of them, was too much. Panic lapped at the edges of Max's consciousness. He didn't know how long he could repel it.

The others were walking ahead of him in single file, but Abby was by his side. He was glad of it. Ever since detonating the avalanche explosives and watching the snow slide down the mountainside, a numbness had settled over him. Where four men had been following them, now there were only three. Max couldn't help imagining the fate of the fourth. The impact of the snow. The crushing dread as it covered him. The desperate struggle to worm his way out, not knowing which direction was up. The gradual realisation that it was hopeless. The body shutting down, starved of oxygen and warmth. This man might have been out to kill them, but Max would not have wished his death on anybody. And he felt responsible. It had been Max's idea to trigger the avalanche. He hadn't killed the man, but he'd caused him to die.

'You didn't have a choice, Max,' Abby said as they shuffled through the snow. 'You know that, right?'

Max didn't answer.

'Any of us would have done the same, if we'd thought of it. You just got there first. Good job you did, otherwise we could all have a nine millimetre in the forehead.'

Max was grateful to her. 'Thanks,' he said. 'It doesn't feel great, but I guess –'

'It's them or us, Max,' she interrupted him. 'That's obvious, isn't it? You think they're going to give up, just because one of their guys died?'

'No,' Max said. 'I don't.'

'So there you have it. I've got a feeling that by the time this is over, there's going to be more than one fatality. Let's make sure it's theirs, rather than ours, huh?' She said it with such ferocity that Max was momentarily taken aback. Abby surged forward so they were in single file again. They continued to forge up the gully behind the refuge hut.

They were walking blindly. Visibility had reduced to little

more than ten metres. Max was horribly aware of the tracks they were leaving in the snow. There was no time to wipe them out. If the assassins were following, the cadets were leaving them clear directions.

The gulley led to a flat, snowy plain. The wind picked up. It moaned all around them and gusted powdery snow into their faces. Max, who was at the back of the line, shouted at the others to stop for a moment. Lukas, at the front, didn't hear, so Sami ran to him to make him stop. They huddled together, occasionally glancing down the slope they'd been climbing.

'We need to know what we're dealing with,' Max said.

'I'd say we have a pretty good idea what we're dealing with,' Abby said. 'Three men who want us dead.'

'That's not what I meant. Are they just following us directly, or have they split up? We're assuming that if we keep moving quickly we'll outrun them, but what if they're playing it smarter? What if one of them's taking a different route and we end up walking straight into them?'

'How are we going to find that out?' Sami asked.

'Walk in a circle,' said Lili. 'Like, a big circle that winds back on itself. If we see their footprints when we meet our own, we should be able to count how many of them there are.'

The cadets agreed with Lili's tactics. Executing them, however, was not so straightforward. It was difficult, with the visibility so poor and the snow blowing in their faces, to be certain which direction they were walking in. Lukas was still in the lead, and Max could only see him dimly in the whiteout. He stopped every thirty seconds or so and looked back, perhaps to check the others were okay, perhaps for encouragement that he was following the right path. It seemed to Max that he was. The circle was large enough for its curve to be subtle. If you didn't know you were following it, you might not know you weren't travelling in a straight line. At least, Max hoped so. If the assassins realised what they were doing, they could counteract the cadets' tactic by lying in wait for them at the start of the circle. He prepared himself mentally for that outcome, though he didn't know what they would do if it occurred.

It didn't. Thirty minutes later they met their footprints again. The wind, still howling, and the blizzard, had covered them somewhat, but they still existed as smooth dents in the snow. More importantly . . .

'Look,' Sami said.

There was no doubt about it. Their trail was busier than when they'd last seen it. There were three distinct extra sets of footprints to the right of the cadets' trail. The assassins were following them as a group.

'They're close,' Lukas said. 'Look, their footprints are almost as well covered as ours. It's taken us half an hour to do that loop, but I think they're much closer behind us than that. Maybe just a few minutes.'

'What are we going to do?' Darius said, sounding panicked.

'Only thing we can do,' Max said. 'Keep going.'

They forged uphill at right angles to the loop. The lack of visibility, Max realised, was a blessing and a curse. Although they could not see where they were going, this meant they were invisible to their pursuers. The only way they could be tracked right now was by the trail they left in the snow. The only way they could be caught was if the assassins moved faster than them. So they kept their pace up, pushing themselves to the limits of their fitness and energy levels.

It soon became clear that they had a problem. Darius was fading. He kept stumbling in the snow. He was supposed to be in between Lili and Sami, but he couldn't move at the same speed and Lili kept catching him up. Each time it happened, she took his arm and encouraged him onwards. But the group could only move at the speed of its slowest member, especially in conditions like these, where to lose visual contact with each other would be disastrous. Max found himself looking back almost as often as he looked forward. Each time, he half expected to see the faint grey outline of a figure in the mist. His back tingled. His natural patience was deserting him. He had the urge to approach Darius and scare him into moving faster, but he suppressed it. Lili's quiet, constant encouragement was a better strategy. Darius could do nothing if he was paralysed by fear.

Gradually the weather worsened. The wind seemed to blow from every direction, kicking up spirals of snow all around them. The blizzard was even thicker than the previous day. Max hunched his shoulders against it and maintained his pace. But then, suddenly, he realised he couldn't see Lukas. He wanted to shout at him to stop, but he couldn't risk it with their pursuers so close. Anyway, would Lukas even hear him above this wind? He ran as fast as he could in the thick snow, past Abby, past Lili and Darius, past Sami. He still couldn't see Lukas, and had to follow his footprints for a full minute before his friend came into view. When he reached him, he put one hand on his shoulder. Lukas started and spun around, apparently ready to fight. He held back when he saw it was Max, then peered beyond him and realised that the others were out of sight. He swore. 'I was going too fast,' he said. He had to shout a little over the wind, even though Max was close. 'I could have lost you.'

'It's easy to do,' Max shouted back. 'But I think we should rope up. That way, we're sure of sticking together.'

Lukas nodded. 'I wish I knew where we were headed,' he said.

'We just need to keep climbing,' Max said. 'Maybe we'll get above the weather, find somewhere to hide.'

They waited for a minute or two in silence while the others caught up. They all agreed with his strategy to rope up. Abby and Sami retrieved coils of rope and carabiners from their packs. It took longer than they would have liked, with their cold, gloved hands, to fix the ropes and carabiners to their harnesses. Each second of delay made Max more anxious, and he kept glancing back, peering through the snow to check there was no sign of the assassins. Once they were secured, with about five metres of rope between each of them, they carried on. Max estimated that they had stopped for five minutes. It meant the assassins were five minutes closer. He wished they could move more quickly.

Angel was no stranger to the mountains.

She had completed the Alpine Guide course. She had spent nights at altitude in fierce storms with only a sheet of canvas between her and the elements. She had climbed sheer rock faces and rappelled down treacherous slopes.

But she had never known conditions like these.

It was as if the mountains were taunting them. They had teased Angel and her companions with a few clear minutes and allowed them to see the cadets and their pursuers as dots in the distance. Then they had hit them with conditions more brutal than any Angel had ever experienced. Biting wind whipped up the snow around them. The mist was so thick it seemed to stick to their clothes. The blizzard was like a solid curtain of snow. Under ordinary circumstances, she would not countenance being in the mountains in weather like this.

But these were not ordinary circumstances.

Angel was not cold. The fire of urgency warmed her, and she sensed the same heat in the others. Nobody had spent as much time with the cadets as she and Woody had. They were family. Hector and Alfie's grim determination was reassuring. Angel had always assumed that nobody felt as protective towards the cadets as she did. Now she wasn't sure.

She was glad they had Alfie with them. Hector's old friend was a comforting presence. Without him, Angel was certain they would be lost. Even now, when they could barely see five metres ahead of them, he seemed to instinctively know where they were going. They couldn't find any trails in the snow but, when the outline of the refuge hut loomed ahead of them, she knew they were on course.

They didn't enter the hut. There was no point. They could tell everything they needed to know from the footprints that led to the gully behind. There were two groups. A set of six and a set of three. Alfie pointed at the group of six. 'You see how those footprints are less distinct than the others?' he said. 'They were laid earlier. More fresh snowfall to cover them.'

It confirmed their suspicions. The three men were chasing the cadets.

They followed without hesitation. Angel could tell that they all wanted to increase their pace. It wasn't easy. The night had been long and arduous. Their energy reserves were low. They ought to stop and refuel, but they had limited food supplies and they didn't know what the next hours or days held. It was a question of mind over matter. Their bodies were weakened, so their minds had to be strong.

They followed the trail up the gully. Finally the terrain levelled out. Angel had no sense of direction. She almost had no sense of movement, as if they were hiking on a snowy treadmill. After twenty minutes, Alfie stopped. 'Look,' he said, and he pointed at the footprints. He grinned at Hector. 'Smart kids,' he said. 'They looped around to check if they were being followed.'

Hector didn't return the grin. 'They *were* being followed,' he said. 'And look. They went off in that direction.' He bent down to examine the sets of footprints. 'The levels have changed,' he said. 'There's less difference in the amount of new snow on the two trails. It means the three guys are catching up with the cadets.'

Nothing Hector said could have better inspired Angel to redouble her efforts.

15

Cornice

Max had heard that the Inuits had fifty words for snow. He'd never quite believed it but now, as the terrain changed, he started to understand that not all snow was alike. There was the powdery, sugary stuff they'd found in the middle of the snowpack? There was the soft stuff that would make good snowballs if they were carefree children, not cadets whose lives were in danger. And there was the stuff that crunched under their boots right now. It was crystalline and icy and it resisted their footfall more than the powder they'd been ploughing through previously. It was slippery, and that slowed them down even further. And as the blizzard swirled around them, Lukas once more disappeared from Max's sight. He was glad they were all connected by the rope.

It happened without a sound, without any clue that they were in danger. The terrain had levelled out a little, so for a couple of minutes they had not been climbing. The rope tightened and tugged at Max's harness. He tried to resist it, to stay upright, but he couldn't. He tumbled forward and fell heavily. He slid several metres along the snow. He braced himself, stiffening his core and pressing his hands into the snow. When he came to a halt, the rope was creaking and straining, and he heard Sami's voice above the wind: 'Lukas! Lukas, where are you?'

Lukas, wherever he was, did not reply.

Think! What could be pulling on the rope? It had to be Lukas himself. Had he fallen? Max squinted through the snow, desperately trying to see ahead. All he could see was Lili, face down in the snow like him.

He couldn't allow himself to move forward. If Lukas had fallen, he could be suspended in mid-air. Any forward movement could cause Sami to fall too.

'Pull back!' he shouted. His voice was hoarse, and he didn't shout at full volume for fear of being heard by the men chasing them. Lili raised one hand to indicate that she'd heard him. Max reached forward and grabbed the rope in front of him. He pulled as hard as he could, gripping the rope as tightly as his numb fingers would allow. It barely moved. His gloves slid backwards along the taut nylon cord.

Another shock of movement. Max glided across the snow another couple of metres before coming to a sudden halt. The rope was straining harder, yanking his harness away from his body. He knew he had to do something before they were all dragged into whatever precipice or crevasse had taken Lukas. Pulling on the rope with his hands was useless. He had to use his body weight. He struggled to his feet, leaning back as much as possible, still trying to grip the rope. Ahead of him, he saw that Lili had come to the same conclusion. She was on her feet, leaning back, pulling hard. Beyond Lili, he could see nothing.

It was like a tug of war against an invisible opponent. The harness dug sharply into Max's back. His arm muscles burned as he pulled on the rope with all the strength he had. Nothing moved except his heels, which dug into the icy snow. He heard Lili shouting. He didn't know what she was saying, but he guessed that she was telling the others – Darius in particular – to adopt the same position. At first, it felt as though her instructions were pointless. The ropes remained under tension but there was no movement in the line. But then Max felt some give. He took a step back – and the line retreated with him.

Another step.

And another.

Little by little, the tug of war became one-sided. It became easier to move back. Then, without warning, Max fell again, backwards this time – a sign that Lukas was no longer in danger.

At least not from falling.

He stood up and hurried forward to the others. Lukas was the last to join them. He was clearly traumatised. His whole body shook, and not just from the cold.

'What happened?' Lili asked.

'I went over a cliff. It was like an outcrop of ice.'

'A cornice,' Lili said. 'Ice builds up over the edge of a precipice. They can be very dangerous. The ice can collapse under you.'

'That didn't happen. I just didn't see the edge. I walked straight over it.' He shuddered at the memory. 'If we hadn't been roped up . . .'

His voice tailed off. Max pointed to the right. 'We need to head in that direction,' he said. 'And quickly. They must be close.'

He was about to lead the way when Abby said, 'Wait.'

'We don't have time.'

'Let's make time,' she said. She stared back at the cornice. 'Did you really not see it?' she asked Lukas. 'I mean, were you just not concentrating?'

'It's like there's another weather system rising up out of the precipice,' Lukas said. 'The visibility at the edge is almost zero.'

'So if the assassins approached the cornice, they wouldn't see it either?'

The wind howled viciously around them as the cadets absorbed the implication of her words.

'How many people do we have to kill today?' Max said.

'We're killing nobody,' Sami said. 'They don't *have* to follow us.'

The fierce expressions on the faces of the other cadets told Max they agreed with Sami.

'They need to think they're following us,' said Sami. 'All of us. We need to leave a trail of footprints all the way to the cornice. Then we can retreat in our own footsteps and move off in a different direction. If the visibility is as bad as Lucas says, we should be able to hide our new footprints well enough to fool them.'

Max didn't like it. If the precipice was so difficult to see, what would stop them falling? If the cornice was just a build-up of ice, what was to stop it collapsing under their weight? And how could they be sure that their new path wouldn't take

122

them to a new cornice? He could see, though, that his friends had made up their minds, and he didn't have a better plan. He nodded at them and they set off.

They kept close. Half a metre between each person. They soon saw that Lukas hadn't been exaggerating. They'd barely advanced fifteen metres when the air seemed to solidify around them. The temperature dropped several degrees and the visibility was so poor that Max couldn't always even see the snow falling in front of his eyes. He felt like each step was a gamble and he couldn't help the image rushing through his head of the six of them, roped together, falling into a misty precipice, surrounded by chunks of ice.

'*Stop!*' It was Lukas's voice. He sounded strained. 'Retreat now!'

Max's breath came fast. He looked over his shoulder, squinting to see his own footprints in the whiteout. They were hardly visible. He wanted to move fast, to get away from the cornice as quickly as possible. But walking steadily was safer, so he forced himself to tread backwards softly.

Five paces.

Ten paces.

Fifteen.

He stopped. Instead of looking at his footprints, he looked behind, peering through the mist for any sign of the assassins. There was none, but they *had* to be close.

'We should change direction!' he hissed at the others, but the wind drowned out his voice and he had to repeat himself more loudly. 'We should change direction! I'll go first! Try to use my footprints.'

He took big strides, moving at right angles to their previous direction. Lili followed, placing her feet in his footprints. He continued like this for fifteen paces, then stopped and waited for the others to join him. Once they were together, he unclipped his harness from the rope and retrieved a collapsible entrenching tool from his pack. He returned through the mist along their footprints. When he reached the second one, he stretched out with the flat part of the entrenching tool and smoothed over the first footprint, like a baker smoothing the icing on a cake. It wasn't a perfect job, but Max calculated that the assassins would be so focused on following the more obvious trail that they wouldn't notice the subterfuge.

He stepped backwards and repeated the process with each footprint in front of him. 'You should go on *Bake Off*,' Abby whispered when he reached the others and clipped himself back into the rope line. Max didn't reply. He thought he could see something through the snow and mist. He held up one finger to indicate that everybody should keep quiet. They fell silent and watched.

The shapes were hardly visible – like a shadow on the edge of your vision that disappears when you try to look at it. They were moving along the trail towards the cornice. The cadets and Darius stood a metre apart from each other, like ice statues. Any movement on their part could attract the assassins' attention. It would not only ruin their tactic. It could be fatal, for the cadets at least. Max held his breath as the grey shapes shuffled past. Only when they were out of sight again did he turn to the others. '*Move!*' he mouthed.

The group needed no encouragement. They headed off, in

single file, roped up, close together. The terrain was rising but the mist around them was as impenetrable as ever.

A minute later, they heard it.

Max might have thought it was the wind howling. He pretended to himself that it was . . . for a moment. But the howl was too human. It was a scream – carried to them, but not caused, by the wind. It faded sharply into nothing, like the siren of an emergency vehicle passing at speed.

The cadets and Darius paused, just for a second. They did not look at each other. They kept their heads down and their shoulders hunched. Then they forged on through the snow.

'*Stop!*'

Alfie's harsh instruction made Woody, Angel and Hector halt immediately.

Woody hadn't imagined that the conditions could worsen. He'd been wrong. He could barely see his companions, let alone his surroundings. He was just about managing to keep at bay the sick feeling of being out of control. He squinted at Alfie, who was paying close attention to the trail they were following. Then Woody bent down to look at it too.

Something had happened here. The trail continued along the same direction, but it also went off at a right angle.

'Wait here,' Alfie said. Without waiting for a response, he followed the original trail and disappeared into the mist.

'What's he doing?' Woody said, unable to keep the frustration from his voice. They didn't need any more delays.

They didn't have to wait long. Alfie returned less than five minutes later. 'Cornice,' he said shortly. Without offering any more explanation, he examined the trails again. Then he stood up straight. 'They approached the precipice,' he said. 'I can't be sure, but I think one of them may have gone over, but they were roped up so my guess is they pulled him back. They retreated from the cornice to this point here, then they went in that direction, hiding their footprints. They let their pursuers follow their tracks to the precipice. I think one of them went over.' He raised an eyebrow. 'Your cubs are growing teeth, Hector. Looks to me like they're picking off their guys one by one.'

Was it Woody's imagination, or did Hector look fiercely proud? Snow had settled on his beard, turning it grey-white. 'Teeth are no good against guns,' he said. 'We need to keep going.'

They kept going.

16

Crevasse

Blue sky.

It appeared without warning. One minute the cadets were struggling up through the blizzard, unable to see more than a couple of metres. The next, they had broken through the clouds. The weather settled beneath them, a bubbling blanket of cloud stretching as far as they could see. The brightness was dazzling, the scenery breathtaking. Snow-capped peaks surrounded them. The wintry sun cast sublime shadows from the peaks across the snow-covered slopes. It felt, for a moment, as if they were the only people on Earth.

Trouble was, they weren't even the only people in the vicinity. There were two others, and they could emerge from the cloud blanket at any moment. And while the conditions had been horrific in the blizzard, they had at least offered the cadets some camouflage. Up here, they could be seen for miles, and it would be even simpler to follow their trail.

There was a cliff about three hundred metres to their one

o'clock. A virgin slope curved uphill to its right. The cadets made for it. There was nothing they could do about the trail they were leaving but, if they could get around that cliff, they would be out of gunsight.

Max was breathing more heavily than normal. The air was even thinner up here. His limbs felt heavier, his movements were more awkward. He forced himself to breathe more deeply. It helped, a little.

It took half an hour to reach the cliff. Looking back, Max saw no sign of the assassins. So they had a thirty-minute lead on them. It was more than Max had expected. The others were breathing heavily too. It was clear that the thin air was affecting them too. Lukas, in particular, looked drained. It was hardly surprising, after tumbling over the cornice. Max felt nauseous just imagining what it must have been like, hanging there, emptiness below him, unable to help himself.

'Mate,' he said, 'let me take the lead for a bit, hey?'

Lukas wasn't the type to accept charity from anyone, but he nodded gratefully and unclipped himself from the rope. Max did the same and they swapped positions.

'I don't know how much higher we can go,' Abby said. 'It's getting hard to breathe, or is it just me?'

Even as she said it, Darius's knees buckled beneath him. Lili was there to catch and support him. Darius staggered to his feet again. His eyes were rolling, but he waved away any further help.

'I'm okay,' he said. His words were slurred. He was obviously very far from okay. He needed rest and oxygen and safety. They *all* needed rest and oxygen and safety. None of these

128

were available to them. So long as the assassins were on their tail and their comms were out, they had no option but to carry on.

Max led them around and over the cliff face. The texture of the snow had changed again. It had a crisp, icy surface a couple of centimetres thick, with soft snow beneath.

'It's like a crème brûlée,' Abby said.

'What the hell's a crème brûlée?' Lukas demanded.

'If we get out of this, I'll buy you one.'

'*When* we get out of this,' Max said. He stopped for a moment and surveyed their position. They were on top of the cliff face now, but set back from it a little. He unclipped himself from the rope, crouched down and shuffled to the edge of the cliff, looking back the way they'd come. The line of their footprints was visible, leading back to the blanket of cloud. As he watched, a figure emerged from the mist. And then, a few seconds later, another. The two men wore black, standing out against the snow. They stopped for a moment and looked around. One of them pointed towards the cliff face. Then they marched onwards, following the cadets' trail.

Max returned to the others. 'They've just arrived above the cloud,' he said.

'So we have a forty-minute lead on them,' Lili said. 'Let's try not to lose it.'

'Roger that,' Max muttered. He clipped himself back onto the rope and carried on walking.

Their route took them to a wide plateau. A hundred metres away, to their ten o'clock, was another refuge hut. It was a good deal smaller than the one they'd entered that morning. Directly in front of them were two sheer cliffs, facing each other, with a narrow gap between them. Their only onward route took them through that gap. There was no need for discussion. Max headed straight for it. They passed the refuge hut and stopped for a moment at the opening of the gap. The cliffs loomed high above them. The gap was about five metres wide, and extended for about twice that length before opening out onto another broad plateau. Max looked back at the others. They were all staring up at the cliff.

'I don't like the look of this,' Abby said.

'Me neither,' said Lili. 'Can you feel the colder air?'

Max could. It was like standing at the mouth of a cave. It was very cold anyway, but between the cliff faces it was colder.

'It's our only route,' he said. 'We turn back, we meet the assassins. We have to keep going.'

He faced the gap. Then he carried on walking.

He suppressed a shiver as the cliff faces enclosed him. He glanced up again as he advanced, unable to shake the idea that the rock faces were pressing in against him.

He was still looking up when the ground moved beneath him. There was a quiet creak, like a door being opened.

Max looked down. A crack had appeared between his feet, the shape of a lightning bolt.

He looked back. The others were staring at him, and at the crack, in horror.

And then the ground collapsed beneath him, and Max was falling.

He knew what it was. A crevasse. A crack in a glacier, covered with snow and ice. Every mountaineer's worst nightmare. It could be hundreds of metres deep. If he hit the bottom, his chances of survival were zero.

He fell, chunks of snow and ice falling with him. It grew darker; he couldn't see the bottom of the crack into which he was plummeting. He felt the rope tighten and he suddenly stopped falling, with a sharp tug on his harness. He swung like a pendulum and smashed into the wall of the crevasse. The impact felt as if it had bruised his ribs and knocked the wind from his lungs. Someone screamed above him. Far below, rocks hit the crevasse floor. He started to spin on his rope as fear hit him and nausea flooded through his body. Desperately, he gasped for air. He reached out, hoping to touch the side of the crevasse and stop himself spinning. His fingertips brushed against rock, but then he was falling again. Hot panic flashed through his brain. He jerked to a halt again, then he was spinning again, and there was nothing he could touch when he reached out. It was grey and gloomy. He looked up. He could just make out the narrow, serrated shape of the crevasse's opening, and he wondered if it was the last thing he would ever see.

It nearly was. More snow and ice fell into the crevasse and something hard hit his head. He blacked out. When he regained consciousness – it could only have been a few seconds later – he was still spinning. His breath was fast and shallow and his nausea had doubled. He reached up woozily and touched the taut rope above him. It felt thin. Too weak to hold him for long. What should he do? Grab the rope and pull himself up? Would that even be possible? Despite his gloves, his hands were numb with cold, and he wasn't certain they would grip. He forced himself to breathe deeply to relieve his panic. It didn't work.

Movement. He was rising. Still spinning, but slowly rising. He reached up towards the top of the crevasse. Its edge was still several metres from his fingertips. He knew he was relying on his friends to pull him to safety. All he could do was hope that they maintained a firm footing, and that their strength did not desert them. He kept looking up, and refused to look down.

It took so long. At least, that's how it seemed to Max as he hung there in the terrifying, freezing gloom. In truth, it took little more than three minutes to haul him to the lip of the crevasse. He saw a gloved hand appear above him. Thankfully, he reached out to grab it. The hand's owner yanked him higher and a moment later Max saw Sami's face, creased with exertion, sweating despite the cold. Max had never gripped someone so hard, nor had he felt so relieved. Sami hauled him back up onto what Max desperately hoped was solid ground.

And then he was lying on his back, gasping in relief, his head throbbing where the falling ice had hit it. His friends were looking down at him. Nobody spoke.

'It's okay,' he said. '*I'm* okay.' He stood up shakily, not certain that his legs would support him. He felt sick again when he saw the crack in the snow. It spanned the width of the gap between the two cliff faces and was at least seven metres long. There was no way of telling how deep it was.

'We've got to cross it,' Max said. 'Somehow. Otherwise they'll catch up with us.'

'It's impossible,' Sami said. 'Look how big it is. And how do we know there aren't more crevasses beyond it?'

'We don't,' Max said. 'But if we stay here or go back . . .' He didn't have to spell it out. They knew what would happen if the assassins caught up with them.

Lukas pointed to the small refuge hut. 'Let's get there,' he said. 'I have an idea.'

Max's stomach lurched with every step. He placed his feet gingerly in the snow, half expecting the ground to twitch and collapse beneath him as it had before. Part of his brain screamed at him to move slowly and carefully. Another part urged him to move fast. The assassins were approaching. To delay could be fatal.

The ground held. They reached the refuge hut. Snow slid silently from the pitched roof as they opened the door and filed inside. There were no furnishings. It was little more than a shed. Boxes of supplies were piled up against one wall, but they didn't have time to rummage through them.

'What's your idea?' Lili asked Lukas.

Lukas pointed to a couple of wooden ladders on the floor. 'One of those,' he said. 'We can use it to cross the crevasse. I didn't understand why they had that ladder in the other refuge hut, but it's what it's there for, I think.'

Max shuddered at the idea. He knew his friend was right, but the thought of returning to the crevasse made him dizzy with anxiety. Abby stood next to him. 'It'll be okay,' she said quietly, and smiled at him.

Max nodded. 'Let's do it,' he said.

They picked up the ladder and shuffled with it back out into the snow. Max looked back the way they'd come. There was no sign of the assassins yet, but they couldn't be more than twenty minutes behind. He forced himself to focus on the crevasse. Max led the others to it with great trepidation. As they reached the edge, they upended the ladder so it was standing upright. Then they let it fall. It slammed down over the hole in the snow, supported by a metre of solid ground at either end. Showers of powder fell into the crevasse and Max suppressed a shudder. The other cadets and Darius were looking at him. As long as he was leading the rope line, he'd have to go first.

'You want to swap?' Lukas said.

Max shook his head. 'When you fall off a horse, the best thing to do is to get straight back on, right?'

Without waiting for an answer, he knelt down on the end of the ladder and gripped the uprights. He took a deep breath. 'Here goes nothing,' he muttered.

The ladder was wooden. It creaked and flexed as Max crawled along it while the others held it in place at the edge of the crevasse. He told himself to look ahead, not down. It proved impossible. He was halfway across and the ladder was bowing alarmingly when, almost as a reflex, he glanced down into the chasm beneath him. His head spun. He gripped the uprights as tightly as his numb hands would allow. The rope offered no comfort. He felt as if he was going to fall. He tried to curl up into a ball, eyes clenched shut, waiting for the vertigo to pass. He heard Abby shout his name, but it sounded distant, as if she was at the other end of a phone line, not a few metres behind him.

The nausea passed. He raised his head and resolutely looked forward, not down. He ignored the movement in the ladder and crawled to the far side of the crevasse. He couldn't feel relieved as he made it to – hopefully – solid ground. The others still had to cross, and there was no guarantee that the ladder would hold. He held the end as Sami scampered across, then Abby. It was Darius's turn next. He was visibly trembling as he ventured onto the ladder and he moved painfully slowly, stopping every half-metre to mutter a prayer and recharge his courage. He made it safely though, which left Lili and Lukas. Lili was cat-like and swift. Lukas was the heaviest. The bow in the ladder was pronounced as he reached the middle. But he moved fast and resolutely, and before long they were all on the far side of the crevasse.

'Let's pull it over,' Max said, 'so they can't use it to cross.'

'We should throw it into the crevasse,' Sami said.

The others murmured their agreement, but Lukas shook his head. 'Pull it over,' he told them. 'I have another idea.' He looked unspeakably grim.

'Whatever it is,' Max said, 'we have to be quick. We can't let them get into firing range.'

'I'll be quick,' Lukas said. 'Don't worry about that.'

It took all of them to pull the ladder safely over. Once it was lying on the snow, Lukas pulled from his pack the Leatherman multitool he had taken from the large refuge hut. He opened the saw attachment and moved halfway along the ladder. He started sawing into one of the uprights. The teeth of the saw were sharp and cut easily into the wood. It took about a minute for him to cut halfway through the upright. He loosened the saw from the wood and repeated the process on the second upright. When it was done, he turned to the others. 'Turn it so the cuts are facing down,' he said.

Silently, they did as Lukas said.

'Now lift it onto its end. Make sure it doesn't fall backwards or it'll break.'

Carefully they lifted the ladder, holding it just before it reached the vertical. Then, on Lukas's instruction, they moved it nearer the crevasse and let it fall over the chasm. They stared at it. Lukas's strategy was suddenly clear to them. The cuts in the uprights had weakened the ladder. The next person who used it to cross would find that out too late. As soon as they approached the centre of the ladder, it would snap, and whoever was on it would take a one-way trip to the bottom of the crevasse. The thought made Max feel nauseous again.

'You're a bad boy, Lukas,' Abby said. She only sounded like she was half joking. 'Clever, but bad.'

'It's them or us,' Lukas said. He turned his back on the crevasse. 'Come on. Let's get out of here.'

Alfie was a bloodhound. He followed the trail in the snow as if he could smell it. The worse the conditions became, the longer his stride. It was as if he was daring the elements to hold him back.

As Hector followed, his mind started to play tricks on him. Perhaps it was the cold, or the thin atmosphere. Whatever the reason, his thoughts kept flashing back with startling clarity to a time many years before when he and Alfie were not surrounded by snow but by sand and dust, their skin wet with perspiration as the brutal Afghan sun beat down on them. They were advancing through the desert towards a cave system where they believed Max's father Reg was being held. Alfie was in the lead, Hector following. There had been something of the bloodhound about Alfie on that day too. His desperation to rescue Reg was akin to his desperation to rescue Max and the others.

As the memories passed through his mind, Hector and the others suddenly emerged above the clouds. A piercing blue sky was above them and all around was a wide, shimmering expanse of snow that made them clap their hands to their eyes to ward off the glare. As they grew accustomed to the brightness, they saw that the trail led past and around a cliff. The footprints in the snow spoke of a group of six and a group of two. Since the blizzard had stopped, there was no way to establish how much time separated the two. They followed, heading up and around the cliff, the bloodhound upping his pace as though the sun on his back had renewed his energy.

Twenty minutes later, Alfie raised a hand. '*Stop!*' he hissed.

They hit the ground. Their bodies sank into the snow as they looked ahead through their binoculars.

They were on a broad plateau. A hundred metres ahead, two sheer cliffs faced each other with a narrow gap between them. Just before the cliffs and to their right was a small refuge hut. Two men in black stood at the beginning of the gap between the cliffs. There was clearly an obstacle ahead of them but, from this angle and distance, it was impossible for Hector to make out what it was.

One of the men crouched down on all fours and advanced.

'It's a crevasse ladder,' Alfie said quietly.

They carried on watching. The man on the ladder was just a dot, moving slowly.

And then, in an instant, he wasn't there.

The remaining guy approached the edge of the crevasse and shouted something. Hector and the others could faintly hear his voice. He stood for a moment, perhaps judging whether he could do anything to help his companion. Then he turned and sprinted through the snow towards the refuge hut.

'What just happened?' Woody asked.

'If I had to hazard a guess,' Angel said, 'I'd say our little cubs just laid another trap.' There was a note of awed pride in her voice. 'They should have been roped together.'

They fell silent again as the guy emerged from the refuge hut. He was struggling with a second ladder, which he carried over to the crevasse. He upended it and let it fall over the chasm, then scrambled across. He didn't look back to check on his fallen mate. He simply disappeared beyond the cliffs, relentlessly following the cadets.

'Do you get the impression,' Woody said, 'that they're doing just fine without us?'

Alfie shook his head. 'Don't get blasé,' he said. 'One guy with a gun can easily take out a bunch of teenagers, even if one of them is Reg Johnson's son.'

'He might have a gun,' Angel said, 'but he's made one big mistake. He's left the crevasse ladder there.'

'I guess that means he doesn't know he's being followed,' said Hector.

'Good,' Alfie said. 'That gives us an advantage – but only if we can catch him up.'

He got to his feet and, without another word, forged onwards to the crevasse. Hector, Woody and Angel followed. They reached it in a couple of minutes, by which time the

138

assassin was out of sight. To their surprise, they found an M16 assault rifle lying in the snow. 'What's this doing here?' Angel said.

Alfie looked at it, then glanced across the crevasse. 'I reckon the first guy to go over left it here to make it easier to cross the ladder,' he said. 'He was probably expecting his mate to throw it over once he'd crossed. But once the first guy fell into the crevasse, his mate didn't want to be weighed down with two weapons.'

'Mistake number two,' Angel said. She strapped the M16 to her body and scrambled over the ladder. Woody followed. They knew the ladder was good, so they didn't waste time roping up. They were already moving away from the far side when Hector turned to Alfie. 'It's good to have you with us, old friend,' he said.

'How about we save the sentimental stuff for when Max and the others are safe?' Alfie said, and he made an 'after you' gesture.

Hector nodded. He crouched and moved resolutely across the crevasse ladder, taking care not to look down. The ladder strained under his weight, but he reached the far side safely then watched Alfie cross. His friend's face was etched with concentration as he moved over the crevasse. Hector turned his back on him when he was almost over, then spun around again when he heard Alfie curse. He had made it to safety, but his leg had become caught on the final rung of the ladder. The ladder pivoted on this side of the crevasse, balanced precariously for a moment, then fell into the crevasse.

The two men watched it fall. Neither of them needed to

state the obvious: that their way back had just disappeared. They would deal with that when the time came. For now, they had more important matters to deal with. They followed Woody and Angel.

They were closing in on the assassin. Surely now it was only a matter of time.

17

The Assassin's Shadow

The cadets were sombre. They were not the types lightly to cause a death.

'We didn't kill them anyway,' Abby said to nobody in particular as they struggled on through the snow. Perhaps, if you looked at it a certain way, she was right. But that was no consolation. Three men were dead. It didn't matter that they would have killed the cadets, given a chance. Life was precious and theirs was gone.

There were other reasons to be fearful. Their journey through the snow was sapping their energy. Their pace was flagging and Max found it difficult to concentrate on effective decision-making. None of the cadets, however, was in as rough a state as Darius. If they hadn't been roped up, he would be trailing far behind them. As it was, he stumbled with every step and fell frequently. When Lili tried to encourage him to his feet, he would stare woozily at her, as if he didn't recognise her. On the rare occasions he spoke, his words were slurred and incoherent. For a while he had been shivering, but even the shivers were subsiding. It was not a good sign. Shivering was the body's way of warming itself up. If Darius no longer had the energy to do that, it meant he was becoming hypothermic. He needed hot liquids and shelter. The cadets needed time to tend to him.

But they didn't have time. They couldn't waste a second. Their only hope was to keep moving. So Lili and Abby practically carried Darius as they struggled through the snow, higher into the mountains. The lack of oxygen made Max's mind as heavy as his limbs. He was finding it difficult to keep track of time. How many days had they been in the mountains now? Two? Three? The blizzard and the mist felt like a distant memory. Even the horror of swinging in the crevasse had faded. He saw himself and his friends as if from above: a bedraggled line of teenagers, half blinded by the snow, stumbling on into the mountains where each step might be fatal, but to stop certainly would be.

Their path had taken them onto another plateau. Its sides sloped steeply away. Up ahead, the terrain morphed into a steep gully. It was their only safe path forward but, when they reached it, their progress slowed dramatically. The snow at the foot of the gully had drifted deeper than elsewhere. It was up to Max's knees, occasionally his thighs. It sucked the remaining warmth from his body and made it almost impossible to move his limbs.

Almost, but not quite. From somewhere, he found a reserve of strength to fight through the snow. And somehow the others did too. Abby and Lili were the most impressive. They managed to manoeuvre Darius up the gully with them, their quiet words of encouragement and formidable strength making up for what he lacked in motivation and power.

They were a hundred metres up the gully when Max raised his head to squint ahead. The top of the gully was half a football pitch away. It opened out onto a rocky peak. It was not clear to Max where they could go after that, even if they managed to reach the top of the gully, which was looking unlikely. The snow was up to his waist now. His legs were creaking to a halt. His body was shivering like Darius's had. He prayed the shivers didn't stop.

He looked back. He blinked heavily. Slowly. Was he seeing what he thought he was seeing? There was no doubt about it. A single figure in black. The cadets had whittled the assassins down from four to one. But one was all it would take to finish the job. The sight of the man lit a fire in Max's core. The guy was approaching the bottom of the gully. He had gained on them.

The others saw that Max was looking down and did the same. There was a grim silence. They looked up the gully. The increasing depth of the snow and the apparently impassable peak at the top meant they had boxed themselves in.

'This is it,' Abby said quietly. 'It's a dead end. We can't get away from him.'

The assassin had stopped too. He raised something to his face and Max knew he was watching them. The assassin lowered his optics and advanced implacably.

'There must be something we can do,' Lili whispered.

Max looked left and right. The sides of the gully were too steep to climb. Their only option was to continue uphill.

The assassin, unhindered by Darius, would move faster than they could. He would catch up eventually. But maybe by then their sluggish, oxygen-starved brains might have come up with a plan . . .

'We have to keep going,' he said. 'We've run out of other options.'

And so they did. It was a strain just to move their legs through the snow. The powder was thick and icy. It resisted Max's movement. He could feel his body seizing up as he desperately tried to wade up the gully and forge a path for the others to follow. He could sense the assassin closing in on them. His back prickled uncomfortably. He wished he could move faster, but his limbs would not obey his brain . . .

'Max!' Abby shrieked. 'Get down!'

If he had been thinking more clearly, he'd have hit the snow immediately. But he wasn't, and he didn't. Instead he turned, and he noticed three things.

One: the others had dived and were buried in the snow.

Two: the assassin was much, *much* closer than he expected him to be. Fifty metres, maximum. He had a long weapon raised.

Three: the red dot of a laser sight dancing on the snow in front of him, moving closer.

He collapsed as the sound of a shot echoed across the mountainside. He didn't know if it was dread or the weakness in his knees that brought him to the ground, or the impact of a bullet. As the snow cushioned his body, he looked down at his chest, fully expecting to see blood. There was none, and he realised he'd hit the ground just in time.

He could see Abby behind him through the path he'd made

in the snow. She was crouching in the snow, hiding Darius's bundled-up form. 'This is it, Max,' she whispered. Her voice trembled with fear. 'What else can we do?'

Max closed his eyes. *Think*, he told himself. *Just think!*

'Max,' Abby said. 'I want to tell you something.'

Max opened his eyes. 'Don't say it,' he said. 'We're going to get out of this alive.'

'No, Max,' Abby said. 'Not this time. We're unarmed, we've got nowhere to run, and we can't move anyway. This is it.' She gave him a sad smile. 'We did some good things, you know. Saved some lives. Helped some people. If I had my time again, I'd definitely choose to be a Special Forces Cadet, even if I knew this was how it might end.'

'We always knew this was how it *might* end.'

'Ah sure, but we never really *thought* it would, right?'

'Right,' Max said. And it suddenly came to him what he had to do.

Slowly and deliberately, he unclipped himself from the rope line.

'Max, what are you doing?'

'No point all of us dying,' he said. 'If I can distract the guy, maybe one of you can get close enough to overpower him.'

'No!'

'Have you got a better idea?'

She looked helplessly at him. 'He'll kill you,' she said.

'Maybe.' He smiled at her. 'Better than him killing you.'

He took a deep breath. Then he stood up.

The other cadets shouted at him to get down. He ignored them. He focused on the gunman. He was closer than when Max

145

had last seen him. Forty-five metres, perhaps, and advancing. He still had his weapon raised and he swung it around to aim at Max, who saw the red dot of the laser sight dance on the snow. He threw himself forward, landing heavily in the powder, which camouflaged him completely as another shot rang out. He heard the others shouting at him.

'Keep quiet!' he bellowed. 'Don't give away your positions!'

Silence.

Max knew that the gunman had to keep advancing if he wanted to overcome the cadets. It would affect the accuracy of his aim. When, a minute later, Max emerged again from the snow, he dived further down the gully but at a different angle. The gunman was closer. Thirty-five metres. He took another shot, but by the time he fired Max was encased in snow again. One more jump, he reckoned, and he would be about two metres from where Lukas was lying out of sight.

He gave it another minute. Then he stood up and dived again. The gunman was twenty metres away. When he fired, the retort of his weapon was definitely louder. The bullet slammed into the snow right by where Max landed.

'Lukas,' he hissed. 'Can you hear me?'

'What are you doing?' Lukas demanded from somewhere behind Max and to his left.

'He knows where I am,' Max said. 'He's going to walk up to me and take a shot at point-blank range. That's your chance. As soon as you hear him fire, go for him. Jump him. Knock him down – do whatever you have to do.'

'Are you crazy?' Lukas said. 'You think I'm going to let him shoot you?'

'You don't have a choice. It's the least sacrifice for the most benefit. You know I'm right, Lukas. Make sure I haven't done this for nothing, okay?'

Silence.

'*Okay, Lukas?*'

'Okay,' Lukas said.

Silence.

'You're the best friend we could have,' Lukas said.

Max had no reply to that. He kept quiet, waiting.

He was shivering. It wasn't just because he was cold. He knew he was doing the right thing, but he was still scared. He remembered the conversation he'd had with Darius, the advice he'd given him. *It's impossible to be brave without being scared first.* It was true, of course, but somehow it didn't help. He wondered what it would feel like when the bullet entered his body. Where would the assassin shoot him? In the head or, more likely, in the chest. Would it hurt? Would he die immediately? What would happen to his body? Would it be left here, high in the mountains, to freeze? Would it be buried in snow when the blizzard returned, as it surely would?

Would he be able to save his friends?

Time slowed. His shivering stopped. He could hear a faint swishing sound. The man moving through the snow. The sound was getting closer.

Max saw the assassin's shadow before he saw the man. It fell across his face as he lay on his back, waiting for his fate.

And then the man himself appeared.

He was tall and broad. His ski gear was black, and he wore a black balaclava that showed only his mouth and his eyes.

His lips were curled in an expression of contempt. His eyes were narrowed. He held his weapon up in the firing position and pointed it at Max's chest.

Max wanted to close his eyes. He didn't. He locked gazes with the assassin. His final gesture of defiance and self-respect.

So he saw it all happen.

Suddenly Lukas emerged from his hiding place and plunged towards the assassin. Max might have known that his friend would ignore the instruction to wait until the assassin had fired. Then Lukas roared loudly to distract the man, and Max knew that perhaps – just perhaps – he had an opportunity. If the assassin wavered just a little, if he moved his weapon away from Max's chest to defend himself against Lukas, then Max could attack . . .

But the assassin was better than that.

Lukas's attempt at distraction didn't work.

The gunman kept his weapon perfectly trained on Max's chest.

A shot rang out.

18

Death Trap

There were so many thoughts in such a brief moment.

Max's first thought was: *It doesn't hurt.*

His second thought was: *He's going to kill Lukas.*

His third thought was: *My plan hasn't worked.*

And then he thought: *Why am I still alive?*

Lukas was on his feet.

The assassin had dropped his weapon.

He was falling.

He slumped heavily into the snow. He fell on Max's legs. Blood seeped from the assassin's back, staining the white snow scarlet. Max scrambled away, half expecting the assassin to twitch into life again. But that was never going to happen.

The gunshot had not come from the assassin's weapon.

It had come from further down the gully.

A woman was standing there. She carried an assault rifle and was in the process of lowering it.

'Angel!' Max whispered. And then he shouted. '*Angel!*'

There were people behind her. Hector and Woody and . . . wasn't that his dad's old friend Alfie Grey? Max couldn't believe what he was seeing. How had they found them? The other cadets were emerging from the snow. Sami and Abby were even laughing. Max avoided looking at the gruesome wound on the assassin's back as he bent down and retrieved the weapon from his fist. It was a submachine gun of some type. Max didn't recognise the make. He stepped around the assassin and shuffled through the snow back towards the Watchers.

Woody and Angel were grinning. Even Hector looked as if he wanted to break out into a smile, if only his stony face would allow it. Lili and Abby were helping Darius through the snow. He looked floppy, as though all his strength had left him. They were flanked by Lukas and Sami, ready to take over if they needed to.

The Watchers all gave Max a gruff hug.

'You had us worried for a minute then,' Angel said.

'You think *you* were worried?' Max said. He suddenly felt light, as if the exhaustion of the past two days had disappeared with the sound of Angel's gunshot.

And then he turned to Alfie Grey, expecting to receive the same friendly grin.

He received nothing of the sort.

Alfie's face was a storm cloud. He was looking at Max and the Watchers with something approaching contempt. 'What are you playing at?' he demanded.

Angel frowned. 'I don't know what you mean.'

'I mean,' Alfie said, 'that the mountains can kill you just as easily on the way down as on the way up. Look!'

He pointed back the way they had come. Max felt his spirits sink. A weather front was advancing, a vast grey mass, obscuring the peaks all around them. Eating them up. Max and the others were at the same altitude as the storm, and they could see it moving in their direction.

Very fast.

Alfie pointed at Darius, who was still being helped through the snow by Lili and Abby. 'What's his condition?'

'Bad,' Max said. Any sense of elation had melted away. 'I think he's becoming hypothermic. He's groggy. Finding it hard to move or even talk.'

Alfie removed his pack and pulled out a flask. 'Warm water,' he said. 'For emergencies.' He strode through the snow to Darius and poured out a cup. 'Drink this,' he said. Darius didn't appear to understand so Alfie held the cup to his lips. Darius drank, just a little at first, then deeply. It seemed to have an effect.

'Can you understand me?' Alfie said, loudly and clearly.

Darius nodded.

'You have to pee,' he said.

Darius blinked.

'I mean it. Your body expends valuable energy keeping your urine warm. You have to get rid of it.' He took hold of Darius's arm and indicated to Lili and Abby that they should let go and step aside. They did. Max and the others turned their backs on Alfie and Darius as Alfie helped the Iranian boy urinate. Afterwards, Alfie returned to his pack, stowed the flask and produced some chemical heat packs. He activated them and helped Darius place them in his gloves and under his arms. All the while, Max watched the weather front. It was almost upon them. The blue sky was hazing over. The air temperature, already low, dropped noticeably. He turned to see how Alfie and Darius were getting on and realised that visibility had already diminished. Darius, however, looked better. As though he'd had an injection of life.

The snow started as Alfie was putting his pack back on. 'Give me that,' Alfie said, pointing at the assassin's submachine gun.

For some reason, Max was reluctant to hand it over.

'Just give it to me, Max. The last thing you need is extra weight to carry. And if we're going to get off this mountain alive, you'd better get used to doing what I tell you.'

'Do it, Max,' Hector said.

Max handed Alfie the firearm.

'We're going to rope up,' Alfie said. 'We move at the pace of the slowest person. That's Darius. He's going to stay with me at the front. Hector's going to take the rear. The rest of you in between.'

They roped up, using an extra coil that Woody had in his pack. Max found himself behind Alfie and Darius, with Angel next in line. By the time they were ready to move, the blizzard had intensified. He couldn't see Hector at the back of the line, and he certainly couldn't see where the assassin's body lay.

'Let's move!' Alfie shouted. His voice sounded strangely deadened by the elements.

Their pace was slow. Even though Darius was in better shape, he still needed Alfie's support. Alfie's reserves of strength were astonishing. He seemed to thrive on hardship, and although he was dwarfed by the mountains, he seemed to have something of their power. His very presence reassured Max, gave him a sense that this final battle with the mountain was one they could win.

They followed their trail back to the open crevasse. By the time they reached it, there was a subtle change in the quality of the light. Evening was drawing in. Time was against them. As they congregated at the edge of the chasm, Max relived the awful moment when he'd found himself hanging inside it. The memory made his legs weak. Could it really only have happened a couple of hours ago? He had to look away.

'How did you cross it?' he asked Alfie.

'Same way as you. Ladder. But it fell just as I got to this side.'

'So what are we going to do?'

Alfie didn't answer immediately. He was examining the cliff faces on either side of the crevasse. The one to their right was sheer and about fifteen metres high, although the top was lost in the blizzard. There were cracks in the rock, deep veins that twisted their random way up the cliff. Alfie was fitting his fingers into one of those cracks, feeling its depth and sturdiness. He looked up. He stayed like that for a couple of minutes while the others shivered around him. Then he turned to them.

'We're losing daylight,' he said. 'There's a good chance some of us might not survive another night on the mountain. Maybe, if we can get to the refuge hut on the other side of the crevasse, we'll have a chance. But there's only one way to get there.'

He pointed to the cliff face. The rest of them stared at it. Were they thinking the same as Max: to attempt a climb like that in conditions like these was madness?

'It's our only option,' Alfie said. 'We can't cross the crevasse, and the approach to the top of this cliff from all other directions is almost sheer ice. But if we get to the cliff top, we can walk along it and then I know a way round that will get us back to the hut. I'm going to climb it first. I've brought the right gear with me.' He removed his pack and pulled out a handful of objects. They looked like metal blocks attached to short sturdy lengths of cable. 'These are climbing nuts,' he said. 'I'm going to insert them into vertical cracks as I climb, and attach them to a rope. Hector's going to remind you all how to belay up safely. Darius needs to come second while he still has strength. I'll get him straight to the refuge hut while Hector sorts out the rest of you.' He turned to Hector. 'You need to send the cadets up next. I want Max to come after Darius. No offence to the rest of you, but I saw how quickly he moved back at the school when Darius was under fire. If the weather worsens there's a chance we might get split into groups. If that happens, I need his help keeping Darius safe while the rest of you adults look after the rest of the cadets.'

Max felt uncomfortable being singled out like this but, if the other cadets were offended, they didn't show it. Alfie looked at them each in turn. 'It's daunting, I know, but we can do it.'

'Isn't it very dangerous, being the first to climb the rock face and putting in the bolts?' Sami asked. He was staring, awestruck, at the cliff.

'Not as dangerous as the alternative,' Alfie said. He was already arranging his ropes, carabiners and climbing bolts. He put his pack back on. 'And anyway, I'm best qualified for the job. Now listen – once I've installed it, the rope will catch you if you fall. But there are still some techniques that will help you preserve your energy as you climb. Remember that climbing isn't really about your arms. You have bigger, stronger muscles in your legs, so use them. Press your body as close to the wall as you can, otherwise you force your arms to take your weight, not your legs. Keep your core muscles engaged. Accept that you're going to be scared, but try to keep moving. The longer you spend on the rock face, the more exhausted you're going to get. And guys, trust me: I've done this a lot. The bolts I insert are going to be secure. They will hold, and you *will not fall*.'

Alfie inspired confidence. He turned his back on the cadets and faced the cliff. He reached out with a climbing bolt and inserted it into a vertical crack in the rock. He moved it down until it jammed tight. Then he attached a carabiner and started to rope himself on.

He moved swiftly up the wall with the confidence of an expert. He almost looked as if he was glued to the rock. Before long, he had climbed out of sight. Max's body temperature was dropping. He marched on the spot to keep warm. The others did the same, except Darius, who was hunched and hugging himself, looking up at the rock face in undisguised panic. Max approached him.

'You'll be okay,' he said. 'Just do what Alfie says. And remember . . .'

'it's impossible to be brave without being scared first.' Darius smiled weakly. 'In that case,' he said, 'I'm going to be very brave.'

'You can do it,' Max said.

And as he spoke, Alfie shouted from high above them. 'Send Darius up!'

Max stepped back as Hector clipped Darius to the climbing rope. Quietly Hector gave the young Iranian boy instructions, pointing up at the cracks in the wall, clawing his hands to show how he should grip the rock. Darius listened intently and removed his gloves. Then, with Hector's help, he gripped a crack in the wall with his left hand.

At first, Max thought it was never going to work. Darius was so hesitant he barely seemed able to rise a metre up the cliff. Once he got going, however, he was more confident than Max had expected. His body looked awkward, his limbs splayed, and of course he did not rise up the wall as deftly as Alfie had done. But he ascended safely, and that was the main thing.

It was Max's turn to approach the wall. He did so with apprehension. It wasn't the height of the climb that scared him. It was the depth of the fall. If Alfie's climbing bolts failed, he'd be revisiting the crevasse. He couldn't help imagining the assassin lying at the bottom of the chasm, his body broken and twisted, covered with pieces of shattered ladder. The image made him hesitate.

'You okay, Max?' Hector said. 'You ready to climb?'

Max mastered his moment of anxiety. 'I'm ready,' he said.

He clipped into the rope and grabbed the same first crack in the wall as Darius had. He found a protuberance for his right foot, engaged his core muscles and pulled himself onto the wall.

Max kept looking up as he climbed. He knew what would happen if he looked down. It was getting much darker and the flakes of snow glowed like fireflies as they settled on his face. The air was silent, the silence broken only by his grunts of effort and the scraping of his boots and the shuffle of his clothes against the rock face. As he climbed, he found himself falling almost into a trance, he was concentrating so hard. Each movement of his arms and legs felt natural. Even though the position of the climbing nuts and carabiners took him directly over the crevasse, even though the sharp edges of the cracks dug painfully into his numb hands, he realised Alfie had skilfully installed the best, easiest route up the wall.

Alfie. He was a good guy. Max hoped that, when they were safely away from here, he might be able to sit down with him and talk about his mum and dad. They might even end up as friends. Max would like that. The cadets and the Watchers were like family to him, but still: it could be a lonely life, and he would like to have another adult to talk to from time to time. Especially an adult like Alfie. Max felt proud that Alfie had singled him out. Proud that he had noticed Max's quick reflexes in protecting Darius from the sniper on the roof of the school . . .

The thought froze in his brain.

Alfie hadn't seen that happen.

He had only found Max and Darius afterwards, in the school library.

Unless . . .

There was only one person who had seen Max save Darius from the sniper. The sniper himself.

Max felt his breath stick in his chest.

Alfie was the sniper.

Could that possibly be right? If it was the case, why had he moved heaven and earth to rescue Darius?

And then it came to him.

What if Alfie *hadn't* been trying to rescue Darius?

What if he'd been trying to kidnap him?

What if that was why he was at the school in the first place?

What if that was why he had let the crevasse ladder fall?

What if that was why he had insisted on Darius following him up the rock face?

Max frowned. It didn't make sense. If Alfie had wanted to kidnap Darius all along, why had he tried to shoot him at the school?

The answer came to him immediately.

He hadn't been trying to shoot Darius.

He'd been trying to shoot Max.

He looked up.

As he did so, he saw the rope above him fall, and he realised that Alfie Grey had just led him into a death trap.

19

A Billion Snowflakes

The bare fingers of Max's left hand were deep inside a fissure on the wall. His right hand gripped a craggy bulge. His feet were stable on a narrow ledge. He tightened his grip as the rope fell onto his head. He felt the carabiner on his harness loosen and he knew that there was nothing to stop him from falling, apart from his ability to hold on. Alfie Grey had just tried to kill him for a second time.

He could not concentrate on why.

He could not concentrate on anything except his own survival.

'Max!' Abby screamed from the foot of the cliff. They must have seen the rope fall. Someone else shouted his name.

Don't look down.

He blocked out his friends' voices and gripped the rock face so hard that he worried the sharp edge of the fissure might cut into his left hand. He peered upwards. It was too dark now, and the snow was too thick, to see the top of the cliff.

He estimated he was halfway up. Should he try to climb back down, or continue upwards? Unroped, either could be lethal. But staying still was not an option.

He told himself to keep calm. If he continued to climb, he could at least see the way up, if only bit by bit. And he knew, rope or no rope, that there *was* a safe route. He'd have to be at the top of his game. Free-climbing a sheer rock face directly above an open crevasse, there was no room for error. He could concentrate on Alfie Grey and Darius when – if – he reached the top.

He identified another fissure half a metre above his left hand. He loosened his grip. Only the ledge beneath his feet and the bulge at his right hand kept him on the wall. Moving his left hand felt like an act of faith. He did it carefully but without hesitation.

The longer you spend on the rock face, the more exhausted you're going to get.

He moved his right foot next, worming it into a horizontal crack. Then his right hand. Bit by bit he ascended. He kept his body pressed close to the rock, just as Alfie had advised, and focused on taking the weight in his legs. When he passed another climbing nut, he knew he was following Alfie's original route, and that encouraged him. Maybe he was able to do this . . .

But he wasn't safe yet.

Just as the top of the cliff came into view through the gloom, Max grabbed a chunk of rock with his right hand. It came away immediately, and a shower of scree tumbled down the rock face. Instinctively, Max looked down to see it fall. The rubble disappeared into the snowy darkness beneath him and

Max immediately felt dizzy at the thought of the crevasse. He groped blindly for another anchor point for his right hand, but there was nothing. Suddenly, his feet had slipped out of position and he was hanging by just the fingertips of his left hand. He felt his skin tear on the sharp rock and an intense pain shot down his arm. His fingertips slipped. Nothing was stopping him from falling but a bare centimetre of contact with the rock face.

His right foot found purchase. Then his left. He groped desperately for another place to put his right hand. His fingertips located a tiny fissure. He had to squeeze them in hard to stabilise himself. His breathing was ragged and panicked, and it took him several seconds to calm himself.

'You can't stop now,' he muttered. 'It's carry on or die.'

He carried on. His hands were agony but he had to block it out. It occurred to him that Alfie Grey might be waiting for him at the top, ready to push him back over the cliff. But Max decided that wasn't likely. He would want a head start to abduct Darius, and he surely wouldn't imagine that Max might free-climb his way to safety . . .

The lip of the cliff was the hardest part of the climb. There was nothing for Max to hold on to. Just snow, thick and icy. He somehow managed to get his chest to the level of the lip and he leaned forward, supporting himself on his elbows. He swung his left leg up so that his heel had purchase at the top of the cliff, then hauled his body over the top, where he lay for a moment, ensconced in snow and gasping with relief. The sky was dark. The blizzard swirled vigorously above his face. Exhaustion threatened to overwhelm him. A little voice in his head told him to just lie there and let sleep come. He ignored the voice. It was perhaps the most difficult thing he had done on the mountain. It took a supreme effort to force himself to his feet and look around.

There were footprints in the snow. Max had expected them to lead along the cliff face in the direction of the refuge hut, but they didn't. Instead they headed away from the cliff face and disappeared into the blizzard.

Max had a decision to make. Should he stay here and think of a way to help the others climb the cliff? Or should he chase Alfie and Darius? The safest option was to stay here. No question. There was a good chance that Hector could put in another climbing line, then they could make a plan together. But that left Darius at the mercy of Alfie Grey. It would give Alfie an unassailable head start. He had already shown what he was capable of. But if Max chased them, he would put his own life at risk. He might get lost on the mountain. Alone. And Alfie had already tried to kill him twice; he would surely not hesitate to try again. But if Max didn't chase him, Darius would stand no chance.

That meant Max had no option.

He followed the footprints in the snow.

He figured he had an advantage. Alfie might be fast, but Darius was slow. If Max pushed himself, he had a good chance of catching them. He hunched his shoulders against the elements and sped up. Within seconds, the cliff had disappeared behind him. He could see nothing but snow and the footprints trailing into the grey gloom. The encroaching night pressed in on him from all sides. The gradient of the terrain increased. The thin air and exertion made Max dizzy, but he didn't slow down. Thoughts were tumbling around his brain and his mind was an engine, forcing his body to new heights of exertion. How had they managed to misinterpret Alfie's intentions so badly? How had he managed to deceive them? Was he working for the Iranians? Had he always been untrustworthy?

Had he deceived Max's parents in the same way?

It was that thought, more than any other, that kept him going. The slope was getting steeper, the night darker, the temperature lower. He was lost. The footprints ahead and behind were his only means of orientating himself. Soon the way back to the others would be obscured by darkness and fresh snowfall. It was already becoming difficult to see the prints. But his anger at the thought that his parents might have put their trust in the wrong person was like a floodlight illuminating his path. For a Special Forces Cadet, friendship and trust were everything. It was unthinkable to him that Lukas, Sami, Abby or Lili would ever betray him or each other. Alfie Grey was not the first person who had ever tried to kill Max. It had become an occupational hazard, and was not what drove him on. Rather, the idea that Alfie Grey might have betrayed his mum and dad burned inside him.

He knew that Hector, Woody and Angel would tell him to isolate himself from his emotions. To concentrate on the mission. On Darius. As he forged onwards, he tried to do that. It was not possible. The mission and Alfie's betrayal were intertwined, like the individual strands of a climbing rope. They couldn't be unpicked.

It was fully dark now. Half an hour had passed since Max had left the cliff face. The shadow of night had tightened around him, making it more and more difficult to see the trail. He gradually realised that he could only sense the blizzard by the soft whisper of snowflakes against his face. And then, suddenly, he could see nothing.

Absolutely nothing.

No footprints. No mountainside. Not even his fingers when he held them in front of his face.

He stopped.

Listened.

There was only the faint howling of the wind.

Panic rose in his chest. It hadn't occurred to him what would happen if darkness obscured the trail. He rotated on the spot, desperately peering through the night in an attempt to see something. *Anything.*

There was nothing.

It was as dark as a sealed room.

And getting colder.

He was shivering. His mind felt sluggish. His extremities were numb. He wanted to move, but there were so many reasons to stay still. He thought of cliffs and cornices and crevasses. He thought of avalanches. The mountains were treacherous even in good conditions. At night, in a storm, when he was alone? They were deadly.

He crouched and hugged himself in a fruitless attempt to keep warm. What had he been thinking, going off on his own like this? He had been blinded by anger. And now, the likelihood was that he would pay for it with his life. Because surely he could not survive a night alone, exposed to the elements . . .

There was a rumble in the distance. It was as if the mountain was growling at him. As if it was preparing to consume him whole. Max stood up again, a spark of defiance in his chest. Alfie had told them that the mountain could kill them just as easily on the way down as on the way up. That didn't mean Max should give up without a fight. It could growl at him all it wanted. Max would resist its attack.

The mountain argued back. Not with a growl this time, but with a roar. There was an immense crack of thunder that echoed terrifyingly all around him.

'Thundersnow,' he muttered, remembering the thunder and lightning they had experienced during the blizzard the previous day. Maybe – just maybe – the mountain would attempt to strike him with another flash of electricity. If that happened, it would light up his surroundings for a millisecond, giving him a chance to get his bearings. When it happened, he had to be ready . . .

The formation of a plan, however vague, did wonders for his resilience. His mind felt less sluggish, the terror less all-consuming. He braced himself against the cold and the storm. He tasted the metallic bite of electricity building up in the air, and he knew that any moment now, the lightning would come . . .

A flash . . .

The mountains burned themselves onto Max's retinas. Sawtooth peaks surrounded him. He saw a billion snowflakes frozen in a single moment. He saw the slope ahead of him, and behind him, and the trail of footprints in the snow.

And he saw two figures, one tall, one small, against the

electric sky. They had their backs to him – and they were no more than fifty metres away.

Darkness again. A deafening crack of thunder resounded across the mountainside. The outline of Alfie and Darius persisted on Max's retinas for a few seconds, then faded.

Max had marked where they were. He knew they were close. He narrowed his eyes, hunched his shoulders and ran towards them.

20

The Precipice

It was a risk. Max knew that. He could not be certain that he was on the right trajectory to catch up with Alfie and Darius.

It was a risk he was prepared to take. It was that, or die on the mountainside for nothing.

A minute later, there was a second flash of lightning. It confirmed that Max's sense of direction was good. Alfie and Darius were closer. Twenty-five metres. They still had their backs to him. Max thought they had stopped moving, though he didn't know why. The sky darkened again. The retinal burn faded. Another immense crack of thunder rolled all around.

Max advanced to target.

His head was burning with strategy. The element of surprise was his best friend. The snow muffled all sound. The darkness camouflaged him completely. If he could creep up behind Alfie, he could wrestle him to the ground. Overpower him. Alfie was taller than him, but Max was young and strong. He had a chance at least.

He covered another twenty paces. He felt as if the swishing of his feet through the snow and the crunching underfoot were magically amplified a hundredfold, but the rational part of his brain told him that this was paranoia. Alfie was not expecting to be followed. He thought Max was dead at the bottom of the crevasse. He thought he had an unassailable lead on Hector and the others.

A third flash of lightning lit up the sky.

Max's heart stopped.

He was close. Very close. Five metres.

And Alfie had turned. He was facing Max. Staring at him. His expression, bleached by the lightning, was cold and ruthless. Darius was several metres away from him, looking on in horror. Just behind them was the reason they had stopped: a cornice, hanging over into a precipice so vast Max couldn't see the other side or begin to imagine its depth.

It was not Alfie's face that filled Max with dread. It wasn't even the precipice.

It was the firearm.

The assassin's firearm. The submachine gun that Alfie had made Max give to him.

It was pointing directly at Max, for the second time.

Max's reaction was instinctive, his movement fuelled by adrenaline. He dived to his left as the lightning faded again. He heard the retort of the weapon and, in his peripheral vision, saw its muzzle flash. An ear-splitting crack of thunder exploded around the mountainside as Max hit the snow. He rolled quickly, because he predicted that Alfie would be able to estimate his landing zone. He was right. There was another retort. Another muzzle flash. He sensed the bullet slamming into the snow to his right.

Then the thunder receded. Everything was dark and silent.

He barely dared to breathe. He knew that Alfie would be wondering if he'd hit him. Max's best move was to stay very still.

He did exactly that.

'You're a lot like your dad, Max,' Alfie called. His voice was tight and edgy. There was uncertainty in it. He didn't know if he was talking to a living person or a corpse. 'Slippery. Persistent. He was a hard man to kill too.'

A sensation passed through Max's body such as he had never experienced: a horrible tingling, mixed with sickness, mixed with a leaden heaviness in the limbs. He was sure that if he could see the world around him, it would be spinning.

He was a hard man to kill too.

'Not as hard to kill as your mum. There was a time when I thought she might even succeed in her crazy attempt to rescue your dad from that Taliban cave in Afghanistan. She was plucky, no two ways about it.'

Each word was a bullet drilling into Max's heart. He could hardly breathe. Hardly think.

'Not plucky enough though. Not *nearly* plucky enough. You'd have thought she'd have tried a bit harder, wouldn't you, with a tiny baby waiting for her back home? You'd have thought she'd have wanted to see him again. I guess she didn't want it badly enough.'

Fury. There was no other word for it. It pushed out every other sensation. Max felt he could judge Alfie's position from the sound of his voice. About four metres to his two o'clock.

He could jump up and attack him in a split second. He could let all his anger out. Pummel the man taunting him. Do his very worst . . .

He stopped himself.

It's what he wants you to do.

That's why he's saying all this.

He wants you to give away your position.

Don't move.

Yet.

'I remember when you were born, Max. Worst thing that ever happened to your parents.'

Max clenched his jaw. Anger burned in his veins.

Focus.

Alfie had changed position. Max could tell by the direction of his voice. He seemed to be circling clockwise. Max estimated that he was still four or five metres away.

'Yeah, they were pretty happy in the early days. Then you came along. Ruined everything for them.'

He had done some difficult things in his life. None of them was as difficult as remaining still and silent.

Don't move.

'Your dad thought he was quite the hero. Maybe if he hadn't been so full of himself, I wouldn't have warned the Taliban that his unit was about to raid their compound. Maybe I wouldn't have tipped them off that your mum was advancing on the cave system where they were holding him. But they paid well, Max. Very well. It's amazing what opportunities exist out there for people with our particular skill set. Maybe one day I'll introduce you to my friends, the Iranians. Even I was surprised at the resources they've been prepared to deploy to get Darius back. I'll admit that you and your little friends did a number on the four guys I sent after you. But tell me honestly, Max, did you really think you could get the better of *me*?'

Silence.

'Did you *really*?'

He was suddenly closer. Three metres. Maybe less. His voice came from the area between Max and the cornice. It sounded like he was facing Max.

Hold your nerve.

Lightning.

Max's surroundings flashed onto his retinas again. Alfie was closer than he thought. Two metres, no more. He had his back to the cornice. The submachine gun was raised. It was pointing over Max's head and Alfie was looking beyond him into the distance. Darius was further away. Ten metres? He had his back to them and looked as if he was trying to escape. The blizzard was thick, the snowflakes seemingly suspended in mid-air.

Then darkness.

Max had only a split second to move. He threw himself at Alfie before his enemy had the opportunity to re-aim and fire. He collided heavily with his legs and felt Alfie fall backwards. There was a crack of thunder. At the same time, Alfie released a round from the submachine gun. Max saw the muzzle flash and realised the bullet had discharged harmlessly into the air. He had to disarm Alfie, who was lying on his back in the snow. Max clawed blindly in the darkness. His right hand fell on the cold metal of the firearm, more by chance than skill. He gripped the body of the submachine gun, ripped it from Alfie's grasp and threw it hard towards the precipice. Had it fallen over the edge? Max didn't know. He didn't have a chance to think about it – because now Alfie was fighting back. He seized Max's throat with one strong hand. With immense strength, he managed to wrestle Max and himself to a standing position. Unable to breathe, Max felt a clenched fist strike the side of his face.

And a second time.

And a third.

His legs buckled beneath him. He tried to fight back, to deliver some solid blows to Alfie's solar plexus, to raise his knee sharply into his groin, but he was dazed and uncoordinated. His feeble attempt at fighting back had no effect. Alfie kept hitting him in the face. Max felt blood trickling down his nose – and then he felt Alfie manoeuvring him towards the cornice. Inching him there, pace by pace. Although Max was putting all his effort into the struggle, he simply could not resist Alfie's strength.

He could feel his heels on the edge of the cornice now. The only thing stopping him from falling was Alfie's hand at his throat. It gripped him hard. Too hard for Max to breathe. And when there was another flash of lightning, and he saw Alfie's face for another fraction of a second, with its narrowed eyes and its self-satisfied smirk, he was in no doubt that his mum and dad's old friend was about to throw him into the precipice.

'I won't lie, Max!' Alfie shouted over the subsequent crack of thunder. 'I saw to it that both your parents met their maker. Feels kind of good to collect the full set!'

Max knew he was going to die. He knew there was nothing he could do to stop it. He only had one thought: to ensure that Alfie Grey paid for what he'd done to Max's mum and dad.

172

He didn't struggle.

He didn't fight.

He simply reached out and grabbed a fistful of Alfie's jacket.

And then he leaned back into the precipice, pulling Alfie with him.

They fell together. Neither of them shouted. Max couldn't. Alfie had let go of his throat but Max still couldn't breathe. The sickening feeling of emptiness beneath him expelled all the air from his lungs. Dread and panic ran cold in his veins as his body accelerated downwards in the darkness . . .

And then abruptly stopped.

He hit snow, soft and deep enough to break his fall, though the impact still winded him. He lay, stunned, for a couple of seconds, trying to work out what had happened. Was the precipice not as deep as he'd thought? He had only fallen for a few seconds. He scrambled to his feet, desperately trying to get some oxygen into his lungs. As he straightened up, there was another flash of lightning. It gave him a further snapshot of his position.

He was on a ledge. It protruded no more than five metres from the cliff edge and was about ten metres long. Max was facing out towards the precipice. Again he saw a billion snowflakes frozen in an instant, and the chasm yawning before him into infinity.

And he saw Alfie.

He was only a metre away. He was on his feet . . . and he wasn't smirking any more. His lip was curled and his eyes flashed with anger. His shoulders were hunched. He looked as if he was about to launch himself at Max.

Darkness. Alfie's form glowed and faded on Max's retinas as Max threw himself against the cliff edge. He felt Alfie dive past him and heard the soft thump as he landed in the snow before the sky exploded with thunder. He was able to breathe now. As oxygen suffused his bloodstream, he felt a little stronger and thought a little smarter.

There were two of them on the ledge, with a storm rolling all around. It was kill or be killed. Max had already embraced death once tonight, and that had been once too often. He had to strike first. Hard and fast.

He brushed the fingertips of his left hand along the cliff face as he ran along the ledge, so that he would not accidentally veer away from it and tumble over the edge. He could hear Alfie scrambling to his feet, but he had the advantage. They collided. Max felt for Alfie's hair. He grabbed a clump in his left hand and pulled as hard as he could. He clenched his right fist and hammered it down into Alfie's face. 'That's for my mum,' he hissed. He hammered a second time. 'That's for my dad.' A third time. 'And that's for me.'

Alfie gasped in pain, writhing and struggling. Max wrestled him to the ground. They sank into the snow. Max knelt on Alfie's chest, still gripping his hair. His right fist was still clenched. He rained blows down on Alfie's face, unable to restrain his fury. He was shouting at him. Screaming. He didn't even know what he was saying. He was out of control.

And that was why he lost the advantage.

Alfie was strong. Too strong for Max, who was so obsessed with revenge that he failed to disable his enemy completely. Alfie's hands were still free. He punched Max hard in the guts. His fist gouged upwards into Max's ribcage, and the blow was so sudden and painful that Max let go of Alfie's hair. There was a flurry of snow and ice in the darkness, and then their positions were reversed. Max was on his back and Alfie was kneeling on his chest, his hand back on Max's throat, squeezing.

Max blinked. He was looking up at the sky, and thought he could see lights at the top of the cliff. Lights? Was he seeing things? Alfie was strangling him, and if he didn't do something about it he would lose consciousness . . .

Alfie's free hand was over his mouth and nose, blocking his airways, suffocating him . . .

He was lightheaded . . .

Dazed . . .

He managed to yank his head back and dislodge the hand on his face. Max opened his mouth and, when Alfie's hand covered it again, he bit as hard as he could. Alfie's knuckle crunched between Max's teeth and he roared in pain again. His grip on Max's neck loosened and Max was able to wrestle him off and jump to his feet.

Silence.

Darkness.

Max had no idea which way he was facing, or where he was on the ledge. A single footstep could put him over. He didn't dare move. Then there was another flash of lightning, and he saw just how precarious his position was.

He was at the very end of the ledge. The cliff face was to his right. To his left, precipice. Behind him, precipice. Ahead of him, three metres away, Alfie. His face was battered and bleeding. His lip was curled. He was leaning forward, his arms outstretched. The position of his body told Max that he was about to run towards him and push him off the edge. His eyes were intent on Max. He was going to charge at him any second.

But Max could tell, in that split second of cold, white lightning, that Alfie hadn't seen the rope.

It was hanging down the cliff face immediately to Max's right. Max could see it in his peripheral vision, and he knew in that instant that he hadn't imagined the lights above him. As the lightning faded and the thunder rolled, he reached out and grabbed the rope. He had never gripped anything so hard in his life, and he prayed that whoever was holding the other end was ready to take the strain.

He swung backwards, off the precipice – and he did it just in time.

As Max gripped the rope, hundreds of metres of empty space beneath him, there were three rapid flashes of lightning, printing three images on Max's brain that he would never forget. The first flash: Alfie lurching forward, arms outstretched. The second flash: Alfie, at the end of the ledge, toppling.

The third flash: Alfie falling, his limbs splayed out, into the unknowable depths of the precipice.

Then darkness.

Max didn't know if his enemy shouted as he fell because another roll of thunder masked all other sound – if there was any. He swung back to the ledge, where he let go of the rope and collapsed into the snow.

The thunder faded away. Silence returned.

But not total silence.

There was one, small sound. It was unheard by any other human, and it was deadened and muffled by the snow.

It was the sound of a teenage boy crying.

21

Morning

The hours that followed were a blur.

Max could not have described in any detail how the others helped him up off the ledge. He only had a vague recollection of torchlight above him, of Hector shouting instructions, of fitting the rope to his climbing harness. He was pulled up, rather than climbing up.

He would never forget, though, Hector's expression by torchlight as he put his hands on Max's shoulders. 'Alfie?'

'Dead,' Max replied. He was too numb and cold and exhausted to know how he felt about that blunt fact.

The thundersnow did not subside. There was movement all around him. Barked orders. The flash of torches. They were roped up. Max was semi-aware of trudging back through the snow, lightning flashing overhead and thunder rolling all around them. He was aware of Abby in front of him, and Lukas in front of her, and of the torchlight that lit the way.

But, more than anything, he was aware of the voice in his head. Alfie's voice.

You're a lot like your dad, Max. Slippery. Persistent. He was a hard man to kill too.

Maybe I wouldn't have tipped them off that your mum was advancing on the cave system where they were holding him. But they paid well, Max. Very well.

Since his earliest days in the Special Forces Cadets, Max had believed that the Taliban had kidnapped his father and that both his parents had died in a raid. He knew that Hector blamed himself for the failure of the rescue mission.

Now he knew there was more to it. Alfie had betrayed Max's parents. He'd betrayed Hector. For Max, nothing would ever be the same again.

Time passed. How the Watchers navigated through the blizzard, Max didn't know. All he knew was that, at some point, he was stumbling downhill and he could see the small refuge hut near the crevasse, illuminated by torchlight.

And then they were inside. Max crouched in a corner, numbly watching his companions as they busied themselves around the hut. He was aware of the dull glow of a camping stove. A cup of hot tea was put into his hands. It burned his lips as he drank, but the hot liquid revived him a little and the babble of conversation in the hut became clearer.

'The storm's clearing.'

'Mobile communications back online.'

'Mountain Rescue have been alerted. They know our position. They'll be here as soon as it's light.'

'Number Ten has been informed that Darius is safe.'

His friends approached him, individually and with obvious concern. They asked him how he was. They put reassuring hands on his shoulder. Max barely responded. He stayed in the corner, hugging his knees, staring into the distance, the activity in the hut a confused blur.

You'd have thought she'd have tried a bit harder, wouldn't you, with a tiny baby waiting for her back home? You'd have thought she'd have wanted to see him again. I guess she didn't want it badly enough.

Then Hector approached. He sat down next to Max and didn't speak for a good long while, for which Max was grateful.

'You want to talk about it?' he said finally.

It turned out that Max did. He told Hector everything. How Alfie had been working for the Iranians and had been after Darius all the time. How he had tried to kill Max. How he had betrayed Max's parents and Hector in return for money from the Taliban. About their fight on the ledge, and how Alfie had plunged to his death.

When he had finished, Hector remained silent for a full minute. He bowed his head, looking to Max like a person in mourning. For whom? he wondered. For Max's mum and dad? For Alfie? Perhaps for the friendship they had once shared.

When he raised his head again, the old Hector was back. Stern and with a thundercloud face. 'He got what he deserved,' he said. 'I've no time for a man who betrays his friends.'

'It's not true, is it?' Max said in a small voice. 'What he said about them, I mean. How they . . . how they weren't happy after I came along.'

Hector didn't answer immediately. He seemed to be considering what to say.

'I'd never seen them happier than when you were born. Everything they did, they did to make the world a better place for their son. And if they could see you now, they'd be prouder than you could ever imagine.'

Max couldn't be certain, in the dark refuge hut, with only the glow of torches for light, but he could have sworn he saw tears slide down Hector's grizzled face.

There were no more words. Everyone was too exhausted to speak. They huddled in silence in the refuge hut until the night had ebbed away and the slow light of dawn crept in.

They stepped outside. The sky was clear and blue, the snow a blinding, icy white. The events of the night were like a bad dream. Max had never been so pleased to see morning.

Their tracks were no longer visible in the snow. Max couldn't help glancing over at the crevasse between the cliffs, shuddering at the memory of swinging in that great chasm. He tore his gaze away and forced himself to take in the breathtaking scenery. The jagged peaks against the sky, the rock and snow and ice, a lone snowfinch circling high above. Then he looked at his friends: at Lukas, Sami, Abby and Lili gazing around in wonder. At Hector, Woody and Angel, their brows furrowed as they watched over the cadets. At Darius, who wore the shocked expression of somebody who knew he was lucky to be alive.

Minutes later, they heard the distant sound of a helicopter. It hovered into view from behind a nearby peak and settled gently on the snow near the refuge hut. The revolving rotor blades kicked up a huge cloud of snow as the cadets, the Watchers and Darius hurried towards it. Max was the last to board. He took one final look at their surroundings then climbed inside.

Then they were airborne. As they rose into the sky, Max stared out of the window. He could see the Matterhorn in the distance, and the snow-capped peaks of the Alps stretching out to the horizon. But he was searching for something else, and after a few seconds he found it: a treacherous cornice with a tiny ledge jutting out from the cliff below. And beyond the ledge, a chasm maybe a hundred metres deep, filled with snow and with no way out.

He glanced at Hector, who was also looking at the cornice. Their eyes met. Hector gave a nod of satisfaction. Then the helicopter banked, the chasm was out of sight, and they were heading away from the peaks, towards Zermatt and safety.

SPECIAL FORCES CADETS

SIEGE

MISSING

JUSTICE

RUTHLESS

HIJACK

ASSASSIN

Chris Ryan

Chris Ryan was born in Newcastle.

In 1984 he joined 22 SAS. After completing the year-long Alpine Guides Course, he was the troop guide for B Squadron Mountain Troop. He completed three tours with the anti-terrorist team, serving as an assaulter, sniper and finally Sniper Team Commander.

Chris was part of the SAS eight-man patrol chosen for the famous Bravo Two Zero mission during the 1991 Gulf War. He was the only member of the unit to escape from Iraq, where three of his colleagues were killed and four captured. This was the longest escape and evasion in the history of the SAS, and for this he was awarded the Military Medal. Chris wrote about his experiences in his book *The One That Got Away*, which was adapted for screen and became an immediate bestseller.

Since then he has written five other books of non-fiction, over twenty bestselling novels and three series of children's books. Chris's novels have gone on to inspire the Sky One series *Strike Back*.

In addition to his books, Chris has presented a number of very successful TV programmes including *Hunting Chris Ryan*, *How Not to Die* and *Chris Ryan's Elite Police*.

HOT KEY BOOKS

Thank you for choosing a Hot Key book.

If you want to know more about our authors and what we publish, you can find us online.

You can start at our website

www.hotkeybooks.com

And you can also find us on:

We hope to see you soon!